LEG UP

LEG UP

A Lark Davis Mystery — Book One

Annabelle Hunter

Leg Up

Lark Davis Mysteries Book 1

Copyright 2019 by Annabelle Hunter

www.annabellehunter.wordpress.com

Cover Design by Melody Simmons

Editing by Casey Harris-Parks of Heart Full of Ink & Joshua Stabile

ISBN: 978-1-7330325-0-6 (ebook)

ISBN: 978-1-7330325-0-6 (print)

Version: 4.26.19

CHECK OUT THESE OTHER WORKS BY ANNABELLE HUNTER

Lark Davis Mystery

Leg Up

Stir Up

Load Up - To be released in September 2019

Barrow Bay Mysteries

Number's Up - To be released in August 2019

DEDICATION

This book is dedicated to my husband, who never thought I could do this, but paid for me to try anyways. Thank you for loving me and supporting me, even when you thought I was crazy.

To Crystal, who was the first one to tell me that my writing wasn't horrible, and I should keep trying. And then had to read most of those tries.

To Katie, who is always up for reading another. And for being the person who told me that this was my story, no matter what I wanted.

ACKNOWLEDGMENTS

Thank you to all the people who have encouraged me and helped me along this journey. First to my friends, who had to sit through too many brain storming sessions, edits, and "what does this mean?" questions. And, amazingly, never lost patience with me. Then to all the people that were willing to read and give me their feedback. I was blessed with some incredible writers to help me on my journey and I, and the book, are both better for it.

I would also like to thank my editors, Joshua Stabile who sat through hours of editing on the phone explaining why I couldn't do things the way I wanted (he was always right, even when I argued). And Casey Harris-Park, who rode to my rescue and has become one of my biggest supporters.

And as always, I would like to thank my family, for helping, encouraging and being so excited that I was taking this step.

CHAPTER 1

There was a severed leg on my porch.

I would like to say I checked to confirm it was real, or gasped in horror, or called the police, or, heck, even screamed. But nope. I stood there, my chin almost hitting my chest as I looked down at the leg in front of me. Thank goodness Hailey was with her father this week, so they could spend some time together before school was back in session at the end of the month. Good parents didn't let their children see dead body parts. Plus, I didn't have the money for that much therapy.

I wouldn't be here if I'd cleaned out my garage like I promised myself I would. If I had, I could've made it to my truck and driven away without even glancing at my front door. Could this be karma for not unpacking all my boxes? No, that was just silly. I was pretty sure karma for a messy garage wasn't a dead body part.

Thoughts like these were probably the reason I was going to hell.

Checking my watch, I pushed some of my light brown hair out of my face and confirmed I would be late to teach my first riding lesson of the day. This was not the way to start my Tuesday. I looked back down. I was

1

probably going to be late for a lot more than that. Sighing, I texted my morning clients and my working student to let them know I would try to arrive by noon.

I looked at the leg again. Could it be fake? I mean, who gets a limb on their doorstep without the corresponding body? Inching forward and holding my breath, I looked closer. Yep. Definitely real. It already smelled enough that I didn't need to breathe for the stench to hit me.

Hmm. I wondered how long it would take for the cops to get here? I heard about how slow the response time was, but I would think a body part would rank high enough to get them here sooner than... I looked at my phone and swore. *Shiitake mushrooms.*

Dialing 911, I waited through the hold message until a female voice came on the line.

"Nine-one-one, what's your emergency?"

"Severed leg."

"Excuse me?"

"I found a severed leg."

"Is it still bleeding? Do you hear noises coming from nearby that might indicate where the owner of the leg is?"

I looked down. I hadn't moved since opening the door, instead my training kicked in, keeping me frozen as I processed. After years of working with horses, it was amazing how quickly I learned to stay calm and still, especially when facing an animal who was depending on me to tell it what to do. And panic was never the right answer. Yeah, I had learned to stay outwardly serene during a crisis. But I had yet to learn how to stop myself from being sarcastic when panicked. I really needed to, though.

"Nope. It's stopped bleeding, and there's no puddle of blood underneath it, so I would guess the previous owner is not around."

"Previous owner?"

"The dead guy."

"Do you know he is dead?"

"Well, there's a leg sitting on my front porch, so unless a hospital around here had a thigh amputation and got remarkably careless with the body part, I would guess the person it came from is dead."

"Ma'am, we ask that you give us the facts and not any assumptions." Well, that came off irritated.

"Okay. I opened my door and there was a severed leg on my porch."

"And you are sure it is human?"

"Yes. I'm sure."

"May I ask how?"

"Well, the shoe was a good indication, but the tattoo really clinched it for me."

"Again, ma'am, we ask for just the facts."

The operator was telling me to hold the sarcasm. Probably a good call. If only I could.

"When can the cops get here?"

"We have a unit en route now."

"Thank you. Can I hang up now? I have things to reschedule. And a garage to clean."

"A garage?"

"It doesn't matter. Can I go?"

"No. I need your name and your address."

"Larklyn Davis." I rattled off my address. "Wait. If I just gave you my address how did you have a unit en route?"

"Are you sure you're not in any danger?" She asked.

"Other than from my homeowner's association fining me for this, yes. I'm safe," I muttered.

Today. The garage would get cleaned today.

"Has the homeowner's association made threats in the past towards your safety?"

"What? No! They'll just... you know what? I'm hanging up now. Thank you for sending the cops." I hung up before she could ask me any more questions I would probably answer sarcastically. I ducked back inside the house and pulled a chair out to sit down, keeping an eye on the leg just in case. From inside my house, even with the door open, the smell wasn't too horrible, so I guessed whoever the leg belonged to hadn't been dead long. My phone rang, and I looked down at it. Missy, my working student, was calling. I gave her lessons in trade for doing all the jobs I didn't want to do. In other words, I couldn't live without her.

"Hey, Missy."

"You texted you'll be late. You never miss lessons. What happened?" Her voice was concerned, and I sighed. She was right, I couldn't afford to miss any paid lessons.

"Severed leg."

"Damn. Did the vet ask you to hold another horse from next door again?"

My next-door neighbors at the stable, while nice people, were awful animal owners. No matter how many times I explained to them what kind of fence to use for horses versus other animals, they insisted on using regular chain link. Since they used the same vet as me, it inevitably ended up with them coming to the barn, wringing their hands and pleading for me to come help. And, the sucker for a horse in distress that I am, I always do.

"Not this time. Human leg."

"You found a human leg?"

"To be more accurate, someone delivered a human leg to my front door."

"I didn't know Amazon got into the body parts business." Horse people. We had a morbid sense of humor.

"Thank goodness they don't. Imagine if it had been in a box? I would have just brought it in, gone to work, and it would have taken days to get rid of the smell."

"We're going to hell, aren't we?" Missy stated.

"I debated driving off before calling the cops. This conversation is just the cherry on top."

"So, you're waiting for the cops now?"

"Yep. Something tells me this'll take a while."

"I guess that something is the leg."

"Har har. I'm hanging up now."

"Wait! Schedule?" Missy threw out before I could press the end button. Son of a gun. How was I going to do this?

"Can you take Jill and Katie's lessons this morning and we'll split the fee? Also, let's lunge Donner and Joey. I'll just ride them Sunday to make up for today's ride." So much for my promise to myself for two whole days off this week. I scheduled my work week so that I got Mondays off and, if I got everyone ridden and there was no show, the occasional Sunday. Before this morning, this week had been looking like one of my few short ones. "Hopefully this won't take long, and I'll be there in time to ride everyone else and do my evening lessons."

"Got it. Good luck. Let me know if more body parts show up."

"Go away." I hung up and checked the time again. Five minutes had passed and still no cops. I eyed the leg again. It looked like a man's leg based on the amount of curly brown hair. Creating a thick layer, the hair covered most of the leg, obscuring a tattoo on the back of the calf. The tattoo looked like an eagle perched on a globe. Wasn't that a military thing? I thought for a second before I took out my phone and confirmed. Marines. The leg belonged to a Marine. Or used to. Maybe still? Did bodies keep possession of their parts once dead? I went to google that answer but I stopped myself. Those kinds of searches never looked good. Nothing else about the leg stood out, and I was left without any other clues to whose it was.

My phone beeped, and I looked down to see that the local blog for town news had alerted me to a news article. I read the first line: *Need a Leg up? Larklyn Davis has you covered.*

Son of a donkey's uncle. I opened it up and read.

> *At 7:08 AM Tuesday morning, Larklyn Davis called the state 911 line to report finding a leg on her property. It is*

believea, at this time, she found it while cleaning in her garage, which we all know she needs to do if she ever wants to catch a man again. She also complained of threats from the homeowner's association. We will follow up with more information as soon as it becomes available.

Shiitake mushrooms! My head dropped into my hands. How did Lindsey get all this information? She had to be sitting close to the dispatch to hear the phone call come in. Being a blogger in a town of 1,000 people couldn't be *that* boring. Alright, maybe it was, but she published the article before the cops even arrived. Where *was* Benny? I dialed the direct line for the station and waited.

"Barrow Bay Police Station. Gladys here. How can I help you?"

"Hey, Gladys. It's Lark. Any chance anyone will swing by my house and pick up this leg anytime soon?"

"Lark! Heard you were having a hard morning, hon. How are you doing?"

Deep breaths, I told myself. Just keep taking deep breaths.

"Fine, Gladys. Fine. About the leg?"

"Oh yes. The boys were just listening to your 911 call. Best laugh we've had all day."

Snickerdoodles.

"I don't suppose Lindsey was there when you were listening to it?" The Barrow Bay Police Department was mostly one big room with no walls. Just desks. This led to lots of jokes and camaraderie. It also led to everyone hearing everything. There were no secrets in the police department. It also didn't help that the dispatch was in the center of the room.

"How did you know? Such a sweet girl. I think she has a thing for one of the boys."

No, she had a thing for being the first person to know anything, and then telling everyone as quickly as humanly possible.

"Just a guess. Leg?"

"Oh yes. Chief Jenkins will be on his way."

Good. The police station was only around the corner, so Benny should be here—

"Wait, *will* be on his way?"

"Yes, dear. He needs to finish his coffee first."

Why did I move out of the city again? Oh yes. I wanted to be anywhere my ex-husband wasn't. And personal small-town charm sounded lovely while I was visiting Gran after my mom and dad died. I was currently re-evaluating that decision.

"I don't suppose if I offer him a fresh cup with my special gourmet blend, I might convince him to come out right away?"

"Well, aren't you just a doll? I'm sure that would do the trick." Gladys had embraced the small-town cliché a little too hard, and I had given up trying to get her to stop using pet names within months of moving here. Some things would never change.

"Well then. I'm brewing it for him right now. Will he be here in a few minutes if I throw in a danish?" I didn't need breakfast, but I needed to get back to work.

"I'm sure that would work, dear. You have a better day!" With that, Gladys hung up the phone to go tell Benny about my bribe.

When I moved here with Hailey last year, a year after my divorce and months after the deaths of my parents, I knew trying to have a stable in a town so small would be hard. At the time, simplifying my life and only having what I needed sounded good. Rebellious. Freeing. What utter bull-puckey. The only thing I escaped was having extra spending money.

That wasn't entirely accurate. I was what they termed 'independently wealthy' thanks to my inheritance from my parents. It was how I bought the stable just out of town and my house close to the main street. All I got out of the divorce was custody of Hailey during the week, most weekends as our schedules would allow, and my three horses. The first was my current top mount, and I hoped to show him within the coming year at Prix St. George in the San Francisco dressage show circuit. The second was my old show master, who I used to do lessons. The third was my baby, a four-year-old warmblood mare I nicknamed Twice. As in 'don't make me say it twice.' Or, if no one was around, Shrew.

Twice was really my daughter's horse, and she had hit a 'My Little Pony' stage when it came time to name the barn's newest addition those years ago. Pleading eyes and a happy smile later, my next great mount was named L.D. Twilight Sparkle. I refused to use Twilight or Twily as her barn name, because I was not going to associate her with the show any more than necessary. Princess of

Friendship, she was not. If the stupid mare didn't worship the ground my daughter walked on, she would have been sold in the divorce. Or I would have taken her mother instead. But no. The little mare fought every command but loved Hailey like they were born to be together. And she hated everyone else. She put up with me most days, but we'd argued over who was in charge too many times for me to list her as my favorite.

I had eight other horses in the barn: four in boarding, and four in some sort of training. Just enough to cover my bills for the feed and shavings, but I was hesitant to get in the habit of dipping into my savings. I still hoped that I could make my business work.

Chief Jenkins, or Benny as we all called him, pulled up right about then, and I had coffee and a pastry waiting for him. Coffee was my one indulgence, and I spent the extra money to have my favorite brand shipped to me, even now that I lived in the middle of nowhere. Chief Jenkins also shared my love of all things caffeinated, a habit he says he picked up in the Marines, and his eyes lit up at the sight of the to-go cup in my hand.

"Lark! Always a pleasure to see you!" His large frame moved slowly up the sidewalk. He was older, somewhere in his early 60s, but my favorite of his features were his eyes. There was something about them that pulled you in. They always seemed to be smiling at you, no matter what was happening, as if his good nature just couldn't be contained.

"You too, Chief. I expect you're going to want to take in the leg before your coffee?" I pointed at the offending limb before pulling the coffee back away from him. I had been around long enough to know that this was a negotiation. We didn't do anything the same in this town.

"Ahh honey, you know I can't touch it until the coroner comes and looks."

No. No, I hadn't known that. My shoulders dropped.

"How long?" I asked as I surrendered the cup and my negotiating position.

He took the coffee after carefully placing a sheet over the limb and stepping over it to come in the house.

"About three hours. Dr. Stevenson is on vacation, so we have to call the county coroner."

"I don't suppose I can leave while you handle this? I mean, it's a leg. That is the extent of my knowledge. I could just give you a key to lock up and—"

"No can do. Need to ask you some questions. Investigate and all that. Detective Hernandez is on his way." He watched as I slumped, resigned that I wasn't going anywhere.

"Can't you do the interview?" I pleaded. "I mean, it isn't like I know anything. Do we really have to wait for Hernandez?"

"And step on the toes of my favorite detective after I worked so hard to get him? Nope." He patted my shoulder. "Should have left for work after the call, honey. Would have been able to get some work done before we had time to go find you."

"Isn't it illegal to leave a crime scene?"

"Everywhere else, yes. Here? Well, I know you

aren't stupid enough to kill someone and then report finding their leg."

I turned and walked away.

"Lark? Where you off to? I'm afraid that now that I'm here I need you to stay."

"I'm going to go clean."

"Clean what?"

"What do you think? My garage. So karma doesn't give me another leg up."

CHAPTER 2

It ended up taking several hours for the coroner to get here, and Benny stayed with me the whole time. Being a resort town, winding down for our off season in September, there wasn't much to do in the police department since most of our issues stemmed from tourists. It always amazed me how people would go on vacation and lose all sense of decorum. We had more than our fair share of drunk and disorderlies, vandalism, and even assaults. From the crime logs during the summer months, I would have guessed that we were in a resort town somewhere exotic. Not on the coast of Northern California with little more than a few quaint stores, a few nice bars, and the beach to recommend it.

We managed to get quite a bit of the garage cleaned out, at least enough to get my truck in. It was amazing how loathe I was to get rid of old bits and pieces of tack, but when faced with a severed limb, I snuffed out my hoarder instincts and ended up throwing away a trash bin of old broken pieces. My truck bed was now filled with items I should have brought to the barn ages ago, and I had moved a few boxes inside to unpack later. By noon I pulled my truck into the garage with a happy cheer, and Benny and I were eating lunch from leftovers I had found in my kitchen. I had long since given up on going to the barn and texted Missy to turn out everyone who wasn't ridden so I had a chance of decent rides tomorrow.

"So how is the barn going?"

"Can't complain. Knew it would be hard to start a business in a town as small as this." I threw a chip in my mouth to make sure I didn't complain. Benny had warned me it would be a hard move, but I had waved off his concerns. Nothing like having to admit he was right when I had been the person telling him it would be ok.

"Any more of your fancy clients follow you?"

I frowned at the reminder. When I had decided to move out here, I had six absentee clients that paid exorbitant fees to have me train their over-bred, overpriced, ego-dream horses. Most had promised that they would come with me and I had happily moved here thinking I would still be a big-name trainer. Only two did. As it turned out, ego bragging worked a lot like real estate. Location, location, location. And Barrow Bay was not a location to brag about. But, one of them was unhappy with their new trainer and had been playing around with the idea of bringing the horse to my barn. The new trainer couldn't get it to show the way I had before. They were still flirting with the idea, and I wasn't pressuring them too hard about it. I was trying not to seem desperate.

"Maybe. I have another who is thinking about following after all." I admitted, hoping we might move to another topic.

"What is it you do again?" He rubbed his forehead as he asked, so I couldn't tell if he was serious or teasing me. Either way, my answer was the same.

"I prance around on pretty ponies to music." We had repeated this conversation so often I no longer tried to be technical or professional. No one here understood what dressage was or why anyone would want to pay extra for it. As far as the town was concerned, I danced on pretty ponies. I rolled with it now.

"Ahh, yes. Like in the Olympics."

"Like in the Olympics," I agreed.

"You going to go to the Olympics? You were a big shot trainer down in the Bay area, right?"

"Always hopeful." I ignored the last comment. I didn't want to think about how well I had done when my name was tied to my ex-husband's. My only consolation was that he was struggling without me, too. As it turned out, separately, neither of us were the trainer we thought we were.

"Well, that would be something. How's your Gran doing?"

"Good. She won last night at Bingo and decided to buy a scooter."

"Please tell me she's buying one of those scooters you push with your leg."

"Nope. She showed me the pictures. It's the 'classic' scooter model, white body with a gray seat. Gets 127 miles per gallon."

"127? No kidding?" He scratched his chin thoughtfully.

"Yep. How long before your wife will want one?"

His wife and my grandmother were in the same sewing group, although I had yet to see any sewing being done. Drinking and gossiping, however? They were masters at that.

"Probably by Christmas. With my luck, by then, all of them will be riding around on scooters, getting tickets left and right. I keep reminding Alice we're pillars of the community, but she doesn't seem to care."

His wife, Alice, was my hero. When she started to gray, she dyed her hair different colors until she settled for an amazing light purple that looked fetching with her blue eyes and light skin. She also had insisted on buying one of the new Volkswagen Bugs when they came out in the same color purple as her hair. I wanted to be like her when I grew up.

"I haven't seen her at the coffee shop recently. How's Alice doing these days?"

The coffee shop, Topped Off Coffee Pot, or Tops as the locals called it, and the Dough & Nut shop were the places to see and be seen in Barrow Bay. Tops sold fabulous coffee, and decent pastries and sandwiches. The Dough & Nut shop sold the best doughnuts I had ever tasted, and gourmet roasted nuts, which I didn't think was a thing, but I was wrong. After a month, I was addicted to their honey-roasted almonds just like the rest of the town. It was absolutely a thing.

"She's good. Bitter about the Bingo loss, but I keep telling her it's just like gambling, and if she's going to get mad every time she loses she shouldn't play."

"Does she ever listen?"

"She pats my cheek and tells me she loves me, then

goes to Bingo the next chance she gets."

I laughed because I'd had similar conversations with Gran. Both hated to lose but loved to gamble. I didn't understand. He shared my laughter before sobering up and giving me a long look.

"Thinking about retiring next year," he said, sitting back in his chair as he watched my reaction.

"No! Who would be Chief?" It shocked me. Benny had been the Chief since he came home from 'the war.' I had to look it up because history wasn't my thing, but I had narrowed it down to likely Vietnam. The look in his eyes when he talked about it stopped me from ever asking to confirm.

"I don't know. Hernandez laughed his way out of my office when I suggested it. He told me that this *was* his retirement, and he doesn't need the headache."

That sounded like him. Detective John Hernandez was in his mid-forties, with the dark black hair that he always kept neat and tidy, and dark skin that made him stand out in a town with mostly European descendants. He and his wife, Judy, had moved here a few years ago from L.A., where he had been a homicide cop. Burned out and needing a change of pace, they came up here on a vacation to the resort, and somehow Benny had convinced them to stay. The way I heard it, Judy had joined the Sewing Circle and packed up their things in Los Angeles before John even had time to turn in his resignation. Benny acted slow, but he had a sneaky, manipulative side to him. I would know. He 'helped' me see all the reasons to stay, too.

"You will find someone. You have a talent for it." I

smiled as I said it, and he winked. Just then, we heard a honk outside. Please let that be the coroner.

"Benny? You in there?" We peeked our heads out the door and saw the county coroner, Robert Johnson, calling out to us before he even got his head out of the back of his van. "I heard something about you having a leg?"

"Yep. Right here on the porch," Benny said, coming out the front door, careful to move around the leg. I stayed inside. The smell was getting worse.

"Now why would anyone deliver a leg on the porch? I would think they would at least wait for a signature," Robert joked.

Funny, guys. Funny.

"Okay, the coroner is here. Can I go now?" I asked Benny, fingers crossed.

"We're still waiting on John. He was out talking with the Sheriff's department in Santa Rosa about a drug issue, but he should be back soon."

Yeah, maybe in a few hours. Santa Rosa was over an hour and a half away from here.

"A drug issue?"

"We've been seeing more drugs going through the resort than normal. We're thinking there might be a second supplier."

"We have a first supplier? Benny, there couldn't be more than a thousand people in this town. How do we have a drug dealer?"

"Is there a size requirement for drugs now?" Benny answered, shaking his head. "Because that would be nice. We've had a low-level dealer for a while, mostly here in town, but there might be someone new. We reached out to the sheriff's department recently to see if they could send some resources to help with it."

"Wow. I feel... less secure now." I shuddered.

"Interesting," Robert interrupted. "The leg this morning didn't affect your sense of security, but knowing we have *two* low-level drug dealers does?" He looked at me, waiting for an answer.

I paused. "Yes?" He examined me like a bug under a microscope.

"But the leg didn't bother you?"

"No? I mean, yes? I don't know." I looked at Benny since he had the most experience with Robert. "How do I get out of this conversation?

"Leave her alone, Bob. She doesn't know you're kidding."

In fact, I was pretty sure he wasn't. A smile erased his strange expression, but it still looked forced. Like he was mimicking a learned reaction. It was creepy.

"Of course! Sorry, Larklyn. I was just kidding."

"Oh, okay." My manners wanted me to say it was fine, but my mouth refused to form the sentence. Just then, John pulled up in his car and I rushed over to meet him.

"John! How was your drive?" I asked as we met halfway in between the house and his car. I didn't wait for him to respond. "So where do you want to interview me?" I continued.

"Well, I guess we can do it here. I was kind of hoping we might do the interview in the kitchen, though. Maybe over some coffee?" He tipped his head down, giving me his best puppy-dog eyes.

Sigh. I would not get to avoid the creepy coroner and I would lose more coffee. Today was not my day. Also, I needed to order more coffee.

"Yeah, sure. Come on in. Watch the leg as you go through the door." We walked back to the house, staying clear of the leg-sized lump under the sheet. "Did you want any creamer to go with it?" I asked as I went to the coffee maker to pour another cup of coffee.

"Nope. Like it black. Got used to it that way and now I just can't adjust back."

"Easier and cheaper. Do you want to go back to using creamer?" I asked.

He chuckled. "Not really. So, what happened this morning?"

"Well, I got ready for work like usual. Nothing out of the ordinary. Until I walked out the front door and there it was."

"'It'?" he deadpanned.

"The leg. Are we going to be literal the whole conversation? Because I'm finding out I don't do literal very well." Nope, I was a sarcasm girl through and through.

"Just teasing you." He was at least polite enough to cover his smirk behind a hand.

"Ahh, you heard the call?"

"Sweetie, it would surprise me if that isn't on the internet by dinner time. It was pure gold."

"Shouldn't you be more worried about who the leg belonged to and what happened, than teasing me about my stupidity?" I snapped, unhappy with the thought I might be an internet star for a 911 fiasco.

"No need to be mean about it." He put his hands up as if to fend me off. "So, let's go over what time it was when you found the leg?"

"7 a.m."

"Exactly?"

"Yep. With Hailey gone, I was right on time this morning."

"What did you do after you opened the door?"

"I stood there staring at it."

"What else? Did you scream? Jump? Call 911?"

"Those are all good, solid reactions, and I wish I could say that I did, but I just stood there staring at it. Oh! Then I texted everyone to tell them I wasn't coming in this morning."

"After you called 911, right?" He looked up at me for a confirmation. I looked down at the table.

"Yeah... no. Before. I kind of forgot to call 911 for a little while. I was focused on covering my lessons and—"

"You waited to call 911? How long?"

"I don't know. Five, six minutes?"

"Lark!"

"I thought I had called them! I assumed that I had until I looked at my phone and realized I hadn't actually done it." He shook his head at me, but let it go.

"And after the call?"

"I stayed in the doorway and watched the leg until Benny got here. He covered it with a sheet and then we cleaned my garage."

"Garage?" Another smirk.

"Does it matter?" I snapped.

"No, probably not since you had police presence with you."

"You mean criminals don't invite you over to help them clean up their garages? I thought that was a service you boys over at the Barrow Bay Police Department offered to all the criminals."

"Not a bad idea, actually. You think we could get criminals to do it?" He looked kind of intrigued.

"With the right advertising, who knows." I smirked at him, and he chuckled again.

"Did you notice anyone around this morning that seemed out of place or unusual?"

"Nope."

"Anything that seemed off? Or weird?"

"Nope."

"Okay, then. I think that's everything for today. You'll need to stay with someone else for tonight, or at least until we can get all the evidence collected. This will be a crime scene."

"Wait. Isn't just my porch a crime scene? I can't use the house at all?"

"Just for tonight. I'm sure we'll be clear tomorrow."

"Can I go get a change of clothes?"

"Sure. I can go with you." We both got up and walked back to the master bedroom. "How is Hailey doing at her dad's?"

"She called last night and said it's going okay. She says she misses me but she is having fun with her dad. Seven-year-olds aren't the best conversationalists."

"Nope, I imagine not."

"Can I ask why you and your wife didn't have any kids?" I couldn't believe I asked that. Stupid. I must have lost my brain when I found the leg. "Oh, gosh! That was rude. I'm sorry. You don't need to answer if you don't want to."

"It's fine. We couldn't. Well, I couldn't. I'd seen so much pain and death, I couldn't risk bringing another life into this world. We've thought about adoption, but it's expensive and we aren't sure they would take a couple as old as us."

"You should! You and Judy would make great parents."

He smiled at me and shook his head while turning his back to me as he looked around. The conversation was over. I worked to throw clothing and toiletries in the overnight bag I usually took to shows.

"Okay, I have everything. Let me text Jen and see if she can put me up for the night." I pulled out my phone and texted.

Me: *Can I crash tonight?*

Jen: *Is there wine in this conversation?*

Me: *White or Red?*

Jen: *Rosé. Also rum.*

Jen: *Maybe two bottles of the wine.*

Me: *Bad day at work?*

Jen: *I am a CPA, right? Like with the numbers and shit?*

Me: *Umm, I don't know if I feel qualified to answer that question, on account of the fact I don't actually know what a CPA does. Other than my taxes.*

Me: *And on that note... Have I told you lately that I love you?*

Jen: *Never mind. How's the leg going?*

Me: *Stupid Lindsey. Inconvenient. Next time you get the leg and I'll go to work.*

Jen: *Hmm, pass. See you tonight. With alcohol.*

Jen was the first friend I made after moving here, and she made town life manageable. She did something, hopefully with 'numbers and shit' for several companies from her house. All I really knew was that she hated it, but it paid too well for her to leave. Plus, the job market in Barrow Bay, home to *two* drug dealers, was almost nonexistent. I checked the time. It was almost three. Missy would have already turned all the horses out and ridden all that she could. I was done for the day. Getting a leg delivered should be enough to count for a sick day.

If I left now I could miss the crowds. Grabbing my bag, my clutch, and my keys, I skirted the leg and all the people working around it as I left my house in search of comfort food and enough wine to make us both forget the day.

***

The town of Barrow Bay was a collection of houses, all crammed behind the main street which ran along the beach. On the north side of the town, Main Street ran into the resort, a sprawling facility that was almost the same size as the town. The resort catered to the rich, almost rich, and people who wanted to pretend for a few days. It was surprisingly full all summer. I wish I knew who did their advertising, because it was fantastic.

My house was on the first street back from Main, a cute three-bedroom cottage, complete with a picket fence and roses. Hailey and I fell in love when Gran drove us past it the first time, and the 'For Sale' sign seemed like fate. I learned later that it was more manipulation, and some well-planned timing, but by then it was too late. We had to have it and our new life was born. I walked almost everywhere unless I was going to the barn or Hailey's school, both of which were on the border of the town where land was cheaper.

Main Street had a collection of bars and restaurants on the beach side, and everything else on the land side. Somehow the town had fought off the entry of any big-name chains and still had mom-and-pop stores lining the street, catering to the tourists and locals alike. The biggest was the grocery store, which had a surprising collection of gourmet cheeses and foods, enough to make me, coming from the land of Whole Foods and organic everything, feel at home.

Next to the grocery store was the liquor store, which also doubled as a 'tasting' venue. During the summer it had daily wine tastings of local California wine, but during the off season they expanded their tastings to all the other alcohols. Over the past year, Jen and I had become regulars at these special tastings, and I now had not only a favorite vodka, but rum and tequila as well. All overpriced and hard to get. Another example of good marketing. I really needed to follow their examples.

Next to the liquor store was the yoga studio, were I cross-trained weekly when I couldn't find a reason not to, followed by the gym and a kid's indoor playground that also watched kids for the tourists too cheap to pay for child care on the resort. After that started the gimmicks. The art stores, the figurines, the special branded glasses. If a tourist wanted to buy it, there was a store for it. I didn't go there often.

After grabbing brie, bread, apples, and our favorite wine, I headed over to Jen's. Jen lived two streets back in a newer area, and her house showed it. Whereas mine was all old-time charm, hers was all contemporary lines and trendy beige. She loved it. I hated it. We agreed to disagree.

As I knocked, Jen opened the door and grabbed the wine, then walked away, leaving it slightly open. I watched her bright blond hair bounce as she walked, perfectly groomed into what I assumed was a fashionable cascade of waves. Shorter than me by a few inches, she was still tall enough to carry her curves gracefully, though she never thought that.

"Nice to see you, too!" I called out after her, carrying the brie and my overnight bag into the house. Dropping the bag under a side table in the entryway, I followed her into the kitchen where she was opening the first bottle. "I guess the day didn't improve?"

"I'm a CPA. Not a miracle worker. There is no such thing as miracle math. Nor is it my job to manage department heads when they fail to understand what the word 'budget' means."

"Well, if you ever figure out that miracle thing, let me know. I could use a little miracle math myself."

"I thought you were getting that horse back."

"Still haven't heard anything for sure." I grabbed the glass Jen put in front of me and took a sip. Well, more like downed half the glass, but I had no kid to watch tonight and a leg to forget. On top of all of that, I had the to-do list that the day's unplanned appearance had delayed. I drank the rest of the glass.

"You'll get her. I have faith in you."

"Glad someone does."

"When does Hailey get back from her dad's?"

"Saturday." I checked my watch. "She should call me around seven. I should probably be somewhat sober."

"Boo." She noticed the bag of food I had placed on the counter and looked inside. "Brie? And Gil's French bread? I love you."

"Fresh out of the oven when I got there. I thought we deserved it after today."

"Please tell me you got chocolate."

"Please. Cake or fudge?" I asked, pulling both out of my overnight bag. I had bought them the night before on a whim. The whim now seemed more like fate.

"Both," she answered with a firm nod. We were on the same page.

After we ate the cake and cheese, and drank most of the first bottle of wine, I managed to still be sober enough to talk to Hailey when she called. After listening to her tell me all the fun things she was doing with her father and his latest fling, I was eyeing the wine bottle again. Hailey wasn't impressed with this new one and didn't think she would make it too much longer. The assistant trainer I caught him with left him when the barn started to struggle. It was the little things in life that made me happy.

After consuming the rest of the first bottle and the second, I crashed in the spare bedroom, drunk enough to ignore the dreadful contemporary artwork that Jen loves. Maybe I missed the art appreciation class when I skipped college, but something about modern art's straight lines disturbed me. Maybe it was the disordered chaos. Or maybe that was the feeling I was supposed to get, and I rejected the piece instead of appreciating the emotions it evoked. Either way, it creeped me out.

Blocking everything else out, I tried to focus on the potential of tomorrow instead of the failure of today. Tomorrow was going to be better. It had to be.

CHAPTER 3

The next morning sucked.

Opening my blurry eyes to the chaos of Jen's so-called painting was horrifying. Then my headache kicked in. Why did I think I was still twenty-five? I couldn't drink two bottles of wine anymore. Not if I didn't drink regularly. I made a mental note to either drink more or drink less.

"Lark? You want some Advil?"

"You are a goddess," I groaned. Jen came in with a bottle of water and two magic pills. The pills that turned me into a human again. I swallowed all her offerings and we sat, contemplating the art from hell. "What is that supposed to be?" I finally asked.

"I don't know. My ex-boyfriend loved it and would go on and on about it. I love modern art, but that one? It's complete trash. He took my dislike as proof I 'didn't get him.'"

"So why didn't you let him keep it?"

"It drives the cheating bastard crazy that I have it. Plus, it freaks my mother out, so she stays fewer days when she visits. Last year she even stayed at the resort to avoid it. I will keep it forever for that alone."

"You're crazy. But brilliant." The genius of her plan

was impressive.

"Worse than crazy. I'm out of coffee."

"No."

"Yes."

"Please tell me you're kidding."

"Nope."

"I hate you."

"Please. Like you could survive a day without me. Get a shower and I'll buy you a coffee from Tops after yoga." She patted me on the shoulder and got up to walk out. Yoga. We had yoga today. I wished I had remembered that last night before we drank so much. Cross training after drinking was horrible. But yoga helps too much for me to skip it today. Well, that and Jen being right outside the door to make me feel guilty.

"I will not forget this!" I called after her.

"Shower! You smell!" she called back.

"Brat," I muttered. But I got up, grabbed my clothing, and followed orders.

Clean, almost awake, and smelling like lavender, I found her in the kitchen searching her fridge.

"I have nothing in here that hasn't expired," she griped.

"When was the last time you went to the store?" I asked. She closed the door and turned to face me, biting her lip and looking sideways as she thought.

"Is it a bad sign I don't remember?"

"Jesus, Jen! What are you living on?"

"Pizza. And Chinese takeout. Oooo! I had salad last week, so I had to have gone then."

"You need to work less."

"I know. I just like the money."

"You like the shoes."

"I *love* the shoes."

"I don't get it. They aren't even comfortable."

"Who needs comfort when I can have red soles?"

"Me. I need comfort." I pointed at myself.

"Oh please. Like those riding boots you walk around in weren't just as expensive."

"But they are comfortable."

"You got sores where they rubbed your skin off when you were breaking them in."

"But they're comfortable *now*," I protested in the defense of my thousand-dollar, custom-designed show boots. Maybe throwing shoes at glass houses wasn't the best idea. "Coffee."

"After yoga."

"This is not a negotiation! I want coffee!" I cried as she pulled us out the door.

An hour later I was sweaty, sore, and ready for coffee. Any coffee. Scratch that. At this point I would have accepted any source of caffeine.

"Caffeine. Now," I threatened.

"We need to talk about your caffeine addiction."

"How are you this annoyingly upbeat?"

"I'm a morning person. I'm always this upbeat after this class. Usually you are, too."

"With caffeine. I assumed you were on caffeine, too. It isn't as annoying with caffeine. Without caffeine it is super annoying."

"Stop whining. We will get you your drug of

choice."

"Everyone's drug of choice," I mumbled.

"You know not everyone drinks coffee, right?"

"Heathens. Or they don't know better. I think I read somewhere that they're psychopaths."

"I think you are referring to people who drink their coffee black, and it was an urban myth."

"You are seriously annoying."

"You already said that. Several times."

"Ahhhh!" I stormed away, locating the coffee shop and heading straight there, waiting only for the cars to pass, before forcing my way in. Jen followed, shaking her head and trailing in my wake.

Tops was full of people, some waiting, too many standing in line, and I realized the Greeks had it right. The Gods were cruel. Not that I believed in the Greek gods. Contemplating religion was something only people who guaranteed they wouldn't end up working Sundays got to do. I, on the other hand, had managed to find a show every Sunday for the first three months after we moved here. After the third month, Gran gave up. Which was good, since even during the off season, I was usually at the barn, doing make-up rides or lessons.

I got in line as I watched Laura, the owner of the shop, run around trying to make drinks. Her afternoon helper, Ana, took orders, looking overwhelmed as she ran her hands through her hair, ripping it out of its ponytail, and shooting Laura panicked glances every time she received a complicated order. She took twice as long as usual, and I was irked at Bryan, who had spoiled me with his quick service and happy smile. How could he not have come in today? And how much less busy was the afternoon shift that Ana had gotten away with this level of incompetence?

Bryan's absence had dragged the service almost to a standstill that my uncaffeinated mind wasn't able to handle. I watched as Laura took over the register to let Ana take a break, just as I made it to the front of the line.

"Can I take your order?" Laura asked without looking at me.

"Mocha. Large." My voice brought her head up.

"Lark. I heard you found a leg on your porch yesterday. Do you know whose?" she asked, leaning towards me a little too much for comfort. I liked my personal space.

"Not a clue." That was weird. "Why?"

"Nothing." She wrote my order down and brushed a stray strand of brown hair out of her face, stopping to frantically hand out drinks.

"Where is Bryan?" I asked when she turned back for my money.

"He didn't show yesterday. Or this morning. That makes him fired. So fired that I can't even say how fired. Bastard." Her face turned red and I could see her hands clench at the mention of her best worker and his unplanned absence.

Oops. Guess I shouldn't have asked. She handed me the wrong change and then went back to handing out drinks.

"Umm…"

"What?" she asked, working to fill the next order. When she didn't even look back at me, I took the missing change as a stressed-out barista fee and moved to join the group of people waiting for drinks. Jen stood there, drinking water and looking healthy. Brat.

"Where is Bryan? This crowd looks like it's about to go feral," Jen commented after taking another swig of her water.

"He didn't show yesterday morning or today. It sounded like a no call/no show. Laura said he is fired. Very fired, evidently."

"Didn't show yesterday? You don't think—" Her voice trailed off as she looked thoughtful.

"Don't think what?" I asked, watching the drinks coming up like a hawk. *Please be mine. Please be mine.*

"You don't think Bryan could be the leg, do you?"

"What are you talking about? Of course Bryan isn't the leg. I mean, who would want to cut up Bryan?"

"It disturbs me that the cutting up part is what you question, instead of the killing part."

"My mind disturbs me, too."

"Lark!" Laura called out my name, and I rushed to the front to grab my drink. Holding it close to my chest, I breathed in the fumes like a starving person at a four-course meal. Taking a sip as I walked back to Jen, I could feel the caffeine rushing through my body. It may have been a placebo effect, but it worked, and I didn't mess with things that worked.

I needed three sips before we left the coffee shop for my house, coffee in hand and yoga mats bouncing on our backs. Suddenly, Jen's words made it through the post-morning fog.

Marine tattoo.

"Oh my god. The leg was Bryan's." My eyes met Jen's.

"I told you!"

"Why would anyone want to kill Bryan?"

"I don't know. I don't drink coffee. What was he like?"

"Nice. Happy. Flirty, but not pushy about it. Asked me out once." I thought harder. "Maybe twice. He was around my age, which I thought was weird, but jobs are scarce in town. Drove a car to work."

"He drove a car to work? That's weird."

"Yeah, I assumed that he must live on the outskirts of town at first, but I heard him talking to Mrs. Miller about their shared fence the other day, and she only lives three streets up. Not far enough to drive, I would think."

"He lives next to the Millers? Dang. That's a nice neighborhood."

I frowned at her. "It's Barrow Bay. They're all nice neighborhoods."

"Yeah, but the Millers live in a six-bedroom house with over 4,000 square feet. And the surrounding houses are just as big. How did he afford something like that when he works as a barista?"

"Really good tips?" I guessed.

She gave me a look.

"No one gets tips that good. Maybe he was a gigolo for the rich ladies up at the resort?"

"Okay, I know that we now support two drug dealers, but I'm drawing the line at gigolos. This town does not have gigolos!" I stopped walking for a second to emphasize my 'line.'

"Because drugs are easier to believe?" She raised her eyebrows, daring me to argue. I regretted telling her about them last night during my complaining.

"Because I would be a horrible mother if I had thought about going out with a gigolo."

"So this is back to being about you?"

"Shut up."

"No, really, we should delve into this. What about gigolos offends you?"

"I'm going to work now!" I said as I spotted my silver truck, which somehow still looked reasonably new even though my ex had bought it for me before the split and it had lived through too many horse shows. Jen giggled at me and let me go. "I'll call if they don't give me my house back by tonight," I called out the window.

"Okay! See you later!" she called back as she kept walking towards her house.

I sat there for a moment, contemplating my phone. Should I call the police? I mean, I didn't know for sure. I was just guessing that the leg was Bryan's. And if I guessed this quickly, I was sure the police were already on top of it. Plus, how would it look if I, the unwanted finder of the leg, admitted I suddenly knew who he was? Or thought I knew. Yeah, I didn't think calling John to tell him I might have a guess would end well for me. I would check in with him later to make sure they were on the same track.

The drive out to the barn took about 15 minutes, and I used all of them to contemplate Bryan's likelihood of being the victim. And a gigolo. Please god, don't let him have been a gigolo.

CHAPTER 4

I was finishing up riding my last horse when I saw the car pulling into the barn's driveway. From the flashes I could see through the arena beams, the car looked like John's. Why would the detective come to see me again?

I was riding Twice, and we were close to done, but I decided another few turns around the arena wouldn't hurt. Plus, I kind of liked the idea of being on higher ground when John came in. I was nervous about him showing up, and what it could possibly mean for me. Trying to find my inner peace, I took in the views of my barn, which had quickly become my pride and joy. Because of my hatred of the sun, rain, and really any weather, I had splurged and built an indoor arena. Mirrors lined the far side, and the openings between the ceiling beams allowed me to watch horses play in the turnouts while riding. I could also see my outdoor jumping arena, which I used as a giant turnout in addition to my smaller turnouts. Every morning when I turned out the horses in it, I thought of my ex and how much he would have loved this arena. How he would have spent an hour trying to set up the best jumping course. And then I let the horses play. I didn't even own jumps yet. It brought me glee.

I was enjoying the rocking of Twice's smooth walk when I saw the two men in the mirrors. John's identity I had gathered from the car, but I squinted at the second person. The distance was too far for me to get a good look at him, but I was pretty sure he wasn't from around here. As Twice and I strolled closer to the mirrors, I lost myself in the gentle sway of her back, focusing on the good ride we'd just had, men forgotten. I let myself stay in the moment until I was almost all the way back to the entrance, but was not prepared for what awaited me.

Goodness gracious great balls of Captain America.

I stared. As I processed having a movie star in my arena, my horse drifted to a stop, enjoying an excuse to rest. The newcomer had dirty blond hair, and a square chin that was… well, chiseled. High cheekbones and large, expressive eyes that pulled me in. Now that I was closer, I could see that this man had a small button nose versus Chris Evan's beak, but the hair was definitely Captain America a la the first few movies.

"Miss Davis," Captain America called out. Even his voice was deep and smooth. Mayday, mayday.

"Ms." I corrected him.

"Excuse my mistake. *Ms*. Davis. My name is Brecken Wilson. John and I would like to have another word with you." *Dagnabit.*

"You're a cop."

"Is that a problem?"

Yes. "No."

"Do you have time to speak?"

I urged the horse toward them as I came up with a response. "I need to put this horse away."

"Can Missy handle it for you?" John interrupted.

"Gone." Oh my god. I was having trouble speaking in front of Captain America... no, Cap. I should be calling him Cap. Stupid, stupid nerves. Maybe I shouldn't have ignored men since my divorce. And, if I was going to be completely honest, during most of my marriage. I didn't even remember some of the hormones pulsing through my body right now.

"Well, then. Can we talk with you while you put the horse away?"

That sounded like a great idea. Twice could give me something to concentrate on other than Captain over there. I swung my leg over and let myself drop to the ground, bending my knees to take the impact of landing without a wince. Getting old sucked.

"Sure." I led Twice past them, and Captain kept pace with me as we walked the short distance to the cross ties.

"Can you confirm your name for me?"

Really? John had known me for two years. If I had kept the wrong name up this long, did they really think I would mess it up now?

"Larklyn Davis."

"And that is your married name?"

"Yes. Same name as the kid." Oh my god. What had I said? 'The kid'? I felt like I was in some old black and white western movie with John Wayne. 'The Kid.' Jesus. I had seen handsome men before. My ex was a handsome man. I looked again at him.

Not *that* handsome.

This would be a long, unimpressive conversation.

"'The kid'?"

"My daughter, Hailey. I kept our names the same after the divorce." Two full sentences. Boo-ya.

"You are divorced?"

"Yes." It was wrong that part of me was hoping that question was just from him and not a normal procedural question. Very wrong.

"And what was your relationship with the victim?"

"Leg finder?" I contemplated him skeptically, my forehead scrunched up as I tried to make his question less stupid in my brain.

"No one told you the identity?"

Not officially, no. But I was not about to admit I had a good idea who it was in front of the cops.

I evaded the question. "Well, I haven't looked at my phone since lunch, so I'm behind on the town gossip."

"No one should know yet."

"Then how would..." I stopped, pursed my lips as I counted to ten, then tried again. "Would you like to tell me who the victim is, or is this a guessing game?" Okay, that was not nice. I guess jaded me got mean when flustered. Or maybe I just got mean when cops tried to trap me in word games.

"Bryan Wilson."

"From Tops?" Ha! We got it right! Oh, wait. Poor Bryan.

"From the coffee house," he confirmed. "What was your relationship?"

"Coffee." He looked at me like I was crazy. Which I was. Obviously.

"You only knew him through the coffee shop?" he clarified.

"Yep."

"I have information that says he asked you out a few times."

"Said no."

"Why? He was an attractive guy." Captain studied me, looking for some reaction or piece of information that would help him solve the case. He came up empty. Like Bryan.

"Don't need an attractive guy."

"What do you need?"

"To get this horse untacked. Do you mind?" I had pulled the saddle off, but I couldn't put it in the tack room without him moving. He stared a second before he understood my request, probably because I wasn't explaining everything, or anything really. After he moved, I slipped the saddle on its rack before I came back out and unwrapped her polo wraps. I was old school. Liked the support of a polo wrap over the new boots they had now.

He walked too close to Twice, and I thought about warning him, but my unwanted attraction had made me uncomfortable and it translated into keeping my mouth shut. Recently my mouth had been getting me into too much trouble anyway.

Usually Twice wasn't nice to anyone but Hailey. On most days, I had a pass because I was the one who brought her treats, but that only granted me a grace period and the benefit of the doubt. Today had been a good day, so anything could happen. I learned early in my career to never try to guess what is going on in a chestnut mare's mind.

"Who is the beauty?" he asked.

"Twice."

"Twice? The horse's name is *Twice*?"

"Nickname." God, I sounded like an idiot.

"What's her real name?"

Why was he stuck on this? Did he have radar for embarrassing information?

"She's my daughter's horse." He waited for me to continue, and when I didn't, he reached out to stroke her nose. I held my breath hoping she wouldn't bite. I stopped unwrapping the polo wrap for a second, only to increase my speed, trying to get it off before I needed to intercede.

"She seems to be a big horse for your seven-year-old."

"How do you know my daughter is seven?" Okay, now that he reminded me of the interview games, I was almost hoping for him to get bit, but my daughter's contrary animal seemed to be delighted by the detective's attention. Slut.

"It was in your file." The mare closed her eyes and leaned into his hand. He must have superb hands. I wondered how they would feel—nope. I was not going to think those thoughts.

"I'm training her, but she's in Hailey's name."

"That seems... different."

"The mare hates everyone. Only likes Hailey," I said

with a shrug.

"Even you?"

"Yep."

"And what is the name of such a hateful beast?" Seriously? I couldn't believe he was going to make me say it.

"L.D. Twilight Sparkle." I winced. This mare was the animal least like the fictional character I could think of but rationalizing with a three-year-old was pointless. We hoped she would forget, but no luck there. Hailey couldn't remember my ex-mother-in-law at the time but remembered what she had named the horse. My luck. His smile told me he recognized the name. And the irony. Huh. I wondered how a hardened detective knew *My Little Pony* characters.

"L.D.?" he asked, and I let out a long sigh before answering.

"Lark Davis. It should have been D.F. for Davis Farms, but she bit my ex and then tried to run him over, so he decided she wanted to be just a dressage horse."

"Is that how you usually decide things?"

"Nope," I answered, and he nodded like that made sense, which it didn't.

"Is she any good?"

"Sure." She was good at standing still while my daughter braided and brushed her. Dressage? The jury was still out. But the joke was on my husband. She could jump the moon. I had to get six-foot fences around my jump arena because she kept jumping out of the five-foot ones. I was holding onto that fact for the next time my ex pissed me off. *Here's your next big mount. Oops. You gave her away. Too bad.*

Then again, if she threw me one more time, I'd load her in the trailer and drive her back to him myself. I'd had it all planned out from the last time she put me in the dirt. I'd pull up and call him so he would get there right as I turned her out. Then I'd watch his face as she jumped out, and he'd realize how talented she was. Then I'd laugh and laugh as I watched him try to catch her again while I drank wine. Or champagne. Maybe both? Heck, it was my dream. Let's go with both.

Just then, John moved in closer to Twice, lured by her easy acceptance of the new visitor. She sensed his movement and her ears, which had been so relaxed they had flopped sideways like a donkey, flattened against her head, and the eye away from Captain opened to pin John with a deadly stare. I jumped in between them to give her my own stare, and motioned for John to move away from her, but she seemed unimpressed. So much for my delusion that I was the dominant one in this relationship. Seeing that John was now out of range, she returned to enjoying Captain's attention.

"Did you ever have any problems with the victim?"

Okay then, I guess we were done with the 'getting to know you' portion of this interview.

As I finished gathering the polo wrap I was working on and flipped it over to re-wrap it so it would be ready for the next time, I thought about how I wanted to respond.

"No. But you knew this because the whole town

would know if I had a problem with the victim." I contemplated his sharp suit and shiny shoes that were now covered in a layer of dust. "Have you ever worked in a small town before? I'm guessing you're from the Bay Area."

"Where I'm from isn't important," he snapped at me.

John snorted, but covered up his smile when we both looked at him.

"Yeah. It is. You see, those TV shows and movies that show the quaint little town, where everyone knows everything and such? The ones people complain aren't real? They're lying to themselves, because they are real and you're in one. You want to know anything about me? Ask Lindsey. She runs the town blog. She knows it all and probably some things even I don't."

"How would she know something about you that you don't?" His face showed an emotion for the first time, turning from blank to curious as his eyebrows furrowed at this thought. John snickered at this point and even I cracked a smile.

"Facts are not always Lindsey's forte," I replied.

"Why would I want to know anything that isn't fact?" the handsome cop asked me. I realized I had really puzzled him at this point.

"Because that's the fun. Trying to use all those detective skills to find the truth in the lies. Isn't that what you do?"

"One of the things," he admitted, but his face had closed off again. Except for his eyes, which were contemplating me. He looked like he didn't know what to think of me.

"Then go find Lindsey and bother her. I need to get home." As I finished unwrapping the polo wraps and then re-wrapping them, I brushed past him again to put them away. Mistake. Tingles shot up my arm from the contact and I ended up wishing I had taken more care as my heart, that rebellious organ I hadn't heard from in a while, jumped.

Nope. That was not going to happen. *Get your emotions together, heart.*

"I am afraid that the department insists that we get personal information directly from the source. Hearsay issues and all that."

Cap had some snark in him.

"Too bad. My life is more interesting when Lindsey is telling it."

"I'm sure."

"What department are you with, exactly?"

"Sheriff's." That stopped me.

"Why is the *Sheriff's* Department here?"

"You had a murder and Detective Hernandez asked for help." His reply made me snort in disbelief.

"Detective Hernandez retired here after 20 years on the streets of Los Angeles as a homicide detective. Try again," I quipped.

"This really is a small town." Again, his mask dropped as he looked at both of us with surprise on his face.

"Yep. You can't sneeze without the whole town bringing you hot tea," John added.

"John, that reminds me. How's your wife's cold? I heard she was feeling under the weather yesterday," I asked as I came all the way out of the tack room.

"She's doing good. Just the sniffles. Used it as an excuse to stay home and knit. Your Gran brought over some of her special blend tea. Had her feeling better in no time." He nodded like I had anything to do with it. I snorted at him. Gran was a force of her own. Gramps used to have some influence, but since he died, no one could suggest anything to her. Gran owned the Tea House in town, specializing in loose leaf teas from around the world and high tea in the afternoon, complete with finger sandwiches and doilies. She blamed my coffee addiction on my father and his 'highfalutin city ways' having corrupted me when I was too young to know any better. I thought her tea obsession was nuts. We'd come to an agreement to ignore the insanity of the other's choices.

"This is nice and everything, but can we get back to the leg?" Captain asked, sending us both a glare. He brought his left hand up to flip a page in his book, and my relationship-starved heart fluttered when it noticed there was no ring.

I didn't care. Nope. It was just my stupid heart. I already knew it had bad taste, and we weren't paying attention to it.

"Sure. There was a leg. It was on the porch when I walked out. I called 911 in what could be one of my most embarrassing moments ever and then bribed the Chief to come wait for the coroner with me by offering up coffee and my morning pastry." I put my hands on my hips as I addressed him. "Anything else, Captain?"

"I'm a detective."

"I'm sorry?"

"I'm a detective. Not a captain."

Right… I was not explaining that one.

"I will remember that. Anything else?"

"Yes. The notes say you contacted your clients before calling 911. Can you explain that?"

Son of a biscuit. I really should've had more than one cup of coffee before walking out and finding that leg. Maybe then I would have remembered to call 911 first and not have to explain how my mind works in an emergency to everyone after. The rule was work first, panic second. Usually it was a useful trait.

"I contacted my clients to rearrange my day."

"Excuse me?"

Yep. He had serious doubts about my sanity. I remembered that look on my father's face when I told him I wanted to skip college and become a horse trainer.

"I contacted my clients. It was the first thing I thought of. That I would be late and needed to take care of the people counting on me."

"Do you normally act like that when you find a body part?"

Now it was my turn to stare at him like he was stupid. "Well, as this was my first time, I don't really know what my 'normal' is."

He looked flustered at that.

"Did you tell anyone why you were running late?"

"Maybe Missy?" I thought about it. "No one over the text messages, and she was the only one who called to find out why."

"Who is Missy?"

"My working-student-slash-assistant-trainer. She's working on getting her medals."

"Medals?" As he started to ask, I cringed.

"Do you know anything about dressage?"

"You prance around on horses and have too much money."

I sighed hard. "Then it doesn't matter." I waived away my comment.

"So what medal is she getting?"

"Nope, forget that. It would take too long."

"Because I think dressage is pretty horse dancing?"

Sigh. Basketball players never had to deal with this. "Yes."

"Okay. I can respect that." Huh. This conversation never ended this well.

"Really?"

"Ever heard of Lacrosse?" he asked.

"Maybe? It's a sport—I think." I remembered something about hot guys and short pants. But that might have been football.

"It's big on the East Coast."

"You sure?" Because that didn't sound right. I mean, dressage is big on the East coast, too, but we had still heard of it over here. Then again, he had a point.

"Yep. Huge."

Maybe he did understand. "Interesting. I'll have to look it up." Those of us with rare sports needed to stick together.

He shook his head at this and turned to John. "Have

you heard of it?"

"Nope. It wasn't a school sport, or a professional one," John replied with a half shrug.

"It's both now!" He threw his hands up and addressed both of us. "San Fran even had a professional lacrosse team."

"Had? What happened?" I asked with a smirk.

"Didn't work out."

"Yep. It's *huge*. Sorry we questioned you," I snickered at him. He lifted an eyebrow at me. "Is it in the Olympics?" I pressed further.

He glared. I deserved that.

"I think we're done here." Captain gave us one more glare for good measure, and then left. I really need to remember his name.

"I don't think he likes me," I commented as John and I watched him leave.

"You were taunting him. After he was so nice and everything."

"It was the 'too much money' comment." I scrunched up my face. "I couldn't let it go. You know, dressage is the only horse competition that doesn't have cash prizes. It sucks."

"I'm walking away before this becomes a soap box conversation."

"That's probably a good idea," I said as I unhooked Twice from the cross ties and walked her to the wash rack. "Hey, John? Can I have my house back tonight?"

"Already released it. Gladys should have left you a message on your phone." He smiled and waved as he left the barn.

I followed him out, stopping at the wash racks as I watched them both get in the car. And I absolutely didn't stare at Captain America's butt as he got in. I definitely did not sneak an extended glance or notice the nice cut in his slacks.

I waved to them as they drove off, but only John waved back. Captain America just glared. I guess he wouldn't be asking me out anytime soon. *Shucks.*

I went back to rinsing off my horse. Work paid the bills. Annoying handsome detectives didn't.

CHAPTER 5

After I was done for the day, I texted Jen to let her know I had my house back.

Me: *House was released. I am running away from your scary painting.*

Jen: *Then its job is done. ;-)*

Me: *What? No more wine for you.*

Jen: *Speaking of*

No. She wouldn't. I couldn't. Well, I didn't have Hailey, so I could, but I shouldn't. *Darn it.* I just talked myself into it and she didn't even finish the question. I had a weak soul when my child was away.

Jen: *The Pub?*

Me: *You are a horrible influence. I need to be home by nine. I have to come in early tomorrow to ride extra horses due to missing rides yesterday.*

Jen: *Boo! Ten.*

Me: *Nine.*

Jen: *Hot new bartender…*

Me: *Please! Like I care about men. I am old now.*

Jen: *You are thirty. Everything still works, I assure you.*

Me: *I assure you the new twenty-something hottie is too young. I am not a cougar.*

Jen: *If he is as cute as they say, you could be. If you gained another ten years.*

Me: *Nope. There isn't a level of that hot outside of movies.*

And detectives, evidently.

Jen: *See you in an hour?*

Me: *Roger that.*

An hour? I could do that. Throwing my things in the truck from this morning, I drove for home. I was unreasonably happy about opening my garage door and pulling my truck in, but I couldn't stop myself from glancing at my porch. Just in case.

I was happy to see no body parts.

An hour later, showered and with light makeup, I was ready to go out. As I studied myself in the mirror, I took in my green eyes, accented nicely with mascara, and my brown hair looked more golden brown than dirt brown today. I used to dye it blonder when I was in San Francisco, but since moving here I had let it revert to its natural color, which was somewhere between a dark strawberry blond and brown. Most days it was brown more than it was anything else. I was satisfied with my outfit. Tight jeans that accented my butt with a low-cut black shirt and my only pair of black heels. I was hot-ish. Okay, maybe I only rated a 'looking good,' but I was happy. Pulling my keys off the hook and grabbing my clutch purse, I walked out the front door, heading to the bar by foot.

And I tripped over something on the porch. *Oh god, no.*

I looked down. Sure enough, it was an arm.

Are you freaking kidding me?

I stopped moving and debated how to get myself out of this one. I already 'touched' the body part, so maybe if I stepped out of my shoes, leaving them where they were, I might not contaminate this too much?

Where did I go wrong in life?

This time I didn't mess with 911. I spoke as soon as John answered the phone.

"Hey, John? Would you mind coming over to my house again? And bring your crew."

"Shit, Lark. Again?"

"Well, it's an arm this time. Does that change anything?"

"This is sick."

That was not the word to use right now. It was a good thing I had an iron stomach after years of working with animals that thought it was fun to cut themselves open right before a big show.

"Yeah, okay. Well, this time I tripped over it, but I'm leaving my shoes and going to The Pub. If you need me, you can find me there."

"Lark, you can't—" I hung up. There was no way I was waiting around for Creepy and the CSI team. I hesitated. But Captain would probably come, too... No, I wasn't that desperate. I didn't want a man. Men weren't worth the time or effort. I had already given enough of both to my ex. Even men who looked like movie stars.

I was pretty sure.

Finding new shoes that were... well, sneakers, I

headed back to the door. Turns out all I had were riding boots and these running shoes. Jesus, I needed to buy new shoes. I wouldn't get the pair that just touched a dead body back any time soon. I hesitated and thought about that for a moment. On second thought, I didn't know that I wanted them back. It was worth dipping into my savings to get dead-body-cooties-free shoes.

I was about to walk out the door when John pulled up, a second car pulling in behind him. *Dagnabit.* John got out of his car with a big smile, which only grew bigger as he took in my appearance and my frown. Captain got out of the second car, giving me a suspicious glare as he walked up.

Yes. I did it and then left the evidence on my porch. Multiple times. You caught me. Maybe we could use the handcuffs to—

Oh my god! I was hopeless.

"Why, hello there. Going somewhere?" John said as he sauntered up my walkway.

"Not anymore," I muttered back.

"So, you found the arm this time? I don't suppose this will be a recurring delivery?" John said, still smiling at my expense.

"Do I have to wait for the coroner this time?" I gave him my best sweet, innocent look. His expression didn't change. Maybe sweet and innocent didn't work as well after thirty. Stupid getting older.

"Nope. Just need you to answer some questions and you'll be on your way."

"Good. I have a lot of alcohol to consume now."

Speaking of… I lifted my hand to ask for a moment while I took my phone out and texted Jen.

Me: *Hey, so I have an arm situation. I will be a little late.*

Jen: *No. Please tell me you didn't get a new delivery.*

Me: *Oh… and I need to stay with you tonight. Even with the scary picture.*

Jen: *Can you opt out of the special delivery option? Or is there a request line to switch it from body parts to wine?*

Me: *You are horrible. I have horrible friends. What happened? I had normal friends in the city.*

Jen: *Did you really?*

I thought about it.

Me: *Maybe not. Christy would have gone all Nancy Drew on it. Also, remind me not to tell her.*

Jen: *Oh my god. I just squirted alcohol out my nose. That burns.*

Me: *Laugh it up. I hate you.*

Jen: *Get here and I will buy you the first round.*

Me: *I will as soon as I can.*

"You done with your social life?" Captain asked, as I put away my phone. I lifted an eyebrow at his aggressive tone but stayed passive.

"Well, since I'm going to assume you will need the house tonight—" I looked at John for confirmation and sighed at his nod. "Then, yes. I had to find a place to stay tonight."

"Are you staying with your boyfriend?"

My other eyebrow joined the first. Boyfriend? I thought I had been pretty clear I was not interested in dating anyone the first time we talked. Then again—

"I thought I was having a hot affair with the victim," I challenged him.

"I never said it was exclusive."

Did he just call me a slut?

"Maybe this is too hard for you *city folk* to understand, but around here we are one-person people." John coughed hard. Oh yeah. "Okay, most of the people—" More coughing. John and I needed to have a talk later. "Okay, me. I'm a one-man woman!"

"Well, you said you turned him down. Who did you turn him down for?"

"No one! Been there, done that, got the lawyer bills to prove it. No men."

"Okay, so a girlfriend?"

"Yeah, I'm meeting up with Jen—" They both looked at me with a mix of shock and what briefly appeared as amused interest. I caught myself. "Girl-*space*-friend! My best friend, Jen! You dirty-minded… minded… men!" *Yeah, that told them.* I seriously needed to work on my inner sarcasm. I turned and walked inside the entryway of my house, leaving the door open for them to follow.

"So, no romantic entanglements?" Captain asked.

"No. None. No romance, no roses, no cuddling by the fire, no men."

"Or women."

"Or women."

"Okay. Glad we got that straight."

Really? Because I was feeling pathetic now. "Good."

"So, you were going to meet *Jen*—?" Captain prompted me.

"Jennifer Ward," I answered.

"You were going to meet Miss Ward at a local restaurant?"

"The Pub." That got him looking at me again. Not that I cared. Or could want his attention on me and only me. Because being the center of such intense focus wasn't sexy at all. Did it get hot in here all of a sudden?

"I assume that's a nickname? Like Tops?"

"Nope. That's it. Just The Pub. Joe thinks it gives it pizzazz."

"He's wrong."

"He's British. He doesn't care," I answered. Captain looked at me with his nose crinkled and his head slightly cocked to the side.

"What does being British have to do with the name?"

"It has to do more with him not caring about the name. He says, quote, 'I'm British. If I want to call it The Bar in my local language, I will.' End quote."

"He realizes that we all speak English, right?"

"I dare you to say that to him. Please. When I'm there to watch it. In fact," I went to my purse and brought out twenty dollars, "I bet you."

"I'm guessing he had strong opinions," Captain said, resigned.

"A few," I said evasively. John snickered. Hold it in, John. You're giving away the game.

"I think I'll pass."

"Darn." I put my money away. "Okay, let's get this

over with. What do you need to know?"

"When did you get home?" John asked, all emotion hidden behind his serious face.

"About 5:15."

"And did you check the front porch when you came in?"

"Yep. Nothing there." This got me their full attention.

"You checked the front when you came in and there was nothing?" John repeated.

"Yep." I watched them both take this in and look at each other. I didn't like their expressions. "You guys want to share why you look like that?"

"Well—" John looked sympathetic. That wasn't good. Then he looked at the ground instead of my eyes. *Oh god.*

"Lark, can I ask when your daughter will be back?" Captain asked.

Oh god!

"Friday." My voice was clipped from fear.

"Can she stay at your ex's for longer?"

"Yes." I just had to confess to my ex that someone was leaving me body parts, and pray that he didn't go to the lawyers.

"I would make that call." Captain gave me a look that said he understood it would be hard.

"Do you have kids?" I asked him.

"No."

"Wife? Ex-wife?"

"Long-time girlfriend once. But she is long gone." Oh no. I was way too interested in his answer. "But my sister is divorced. She has issues with her ex and they fight about custody all the time. I get it."

It was hard to imagine anyone 'got it' until they were in the middle of a divorce, but at least he empathized.

"Thanks. Do you guys need anything else?"

"Do you get drug tested when you compete?" Holy segue, Batman.

"Not normally, no. Just the horses." He had opened his mouth to continue but stopped and looked at me in confusion.

"They test the horses, but not the people?" he asked.

"Yep." Even John looked a little confused, so I continued. "What drugs would the humans take that would help? We only care about the horse."

"Steroids don't help the rider?" Captain asked.

"No, not really." More staring. Explanation time. "Okay, so technically, they can test any FEI rider at any time, at competition or at home. So, yes, they could test me for drugs, but they don't. Only at the Olympic level. Maybe at some international events, but I haven't gone to any yet." Maybe next year, with my horse Bob. He may never be Olympic quality, but we could hold our own.

"And you have never been tested?"

"No."

"Have you ever done any drugs?"

"Other than prescribed medication and Advil, no." Drugs and horses didn't mix well.

"And have you ever procured drugs with the intent to sell?"

What the hell?

"No. You think *I'm* a drug dealer?" I pinned John with a glare, and he looked down at his shoes. Yeah, not going to let him get out of it that easy. "John? You think I'm dealing drugs?"

"No. We just had to ask."

"Why?"

"The reason is confidential."

"Oh no. You just accused me of dealing drugs, and I want to know why. Was Bryan dealing drugs?"

"Lark, it's better if you don't know. Lack of knowledge helps you."

"Fine. I'll ask Lindsey."

John winced before muttering, "Please don't."

"She knows nothing. Don't bother. Everything in this case is confidential," Captain answered at the same time as John. We both turned to look at him. He actually believed what he had just said. Poor, poor man.

Ding!

I didn't even need to look to know Lindsey had posted a new article. I just handed the phone to Captain, reading it over his shoulder. His extremely broad shoulders.

> *Giving an Arm and a Leg*
> *At 5:46 Wednesday, Lark Davis got a*
> *jump start on her newest collection as*
> *someone has now sent her an arm and a*
> *leg. Like the leg from yesterday, they left*
> *the arm on her doorstep. However, this*
> *time Lark called the investigating*

detective directly to report the find, a move that has disappointed everyone who got to hear her 911 call from before. We believe that the victim is Bryan Wilson. The barista at Topped Off Coffee Pot has been missing since Sunday after his shift. Laura has no comment, nor are the police releasing any information at this time. We will update you as soon as we have more details.

"You were saying?" I asked as he finished reading, his face red. He ignored me to turn to John.

"How did she get all this information?" he demanded. John was less than impressed with his anger.

"She has double-Ds, good looks, and a flirty demeanor. And she is the Chief's godchild. What Lindsey wants, she gets." John shrugged and leaned back.

I hadn't known about the godchild thing, but it explained a lot.

"That is unacceptable!" Cap stormed away, throwing his hands in the air and muttering to himself. I was impressed that even in his anger he carefully stepped over the arm before continuing back outside to rant in semi-private. Probably not the time to tell him my neighbors listened to everything.

"Why's he here again?" I asked as we watched his tantrum. He even complained like Captain America. He must be a fan of Marvel. I made a note to ask him.

"Off the record?" Code for 'don't tell Lindsey.'

"Always," I replied.

"Bryan was his cousin. His parents made him come when Bryan missed his phone call Sunday night." John turned to walk deeper into my living room, settling in on a couch.

"Bryan was that close to his parents? Wow. Didn't peg him as being, well, close to his family. He never mentioned them."

"Called them every Sunday night. Like clockwork."

"Interesting. Most people do nothing 'like clockwork,'" I quipped.

"Yeah. Must have had an alert or something. Every Sunday, 7 p.m."

"So, you think he was already dead by then?"

"Probably. The leg was too compromised to give us anything—"

"John!" Cap growled at us.

Oops. I guess we weren't supposed to gossip about the time of death.

"Sorry, Breck," John said, keeping his cool in a way I have always envied. Unless I'm on a horse, I lost it when someone talked to me like that.

"Breck?" I asked.

"Short for Brecken." That got me a look from both like I was an idiot. Okay, so I'd forgotten the guy's name, again. I'm sure I wasn't the first one to do that?

"You didn't remember his name, did you?" John whispered when Cap, aka 'Breck,' wasn't looking, watching my face a little too closely. I needed to pull my professional face out when dealing with law enforcement.

"Yes, I did!" Not at all. "Brecken Wilson. Detective with the Sheriff's Department, based in the city. Plays lacrosse. Divorced sister with a kid." Too much information. *Dang.* I overplayed my hand. John just smiled with victory. Then his smile took a vicious turn, as he noticed my *Avengers* movie sitting on the coffee table. After looking from the cover to Brecken and back again, he glanced at me. For the second time this week, not cleaning up had come back to bite me. *Lesson learned.*

"Captain America, huh?"

Shiitake mushrooms! My mistake was calling him Captain during the first interview at the barn. One day I would learn to keep my mouth shut.

"Captain Who? I have no idea what you are talking about."

He chuckled at me, but Captain—no, Brecken— just looked confused. *Thank goa.*

"I don't even want to know what you two are whispering about. Lark, what time did you find the arm?" Brecken asked with a sigh.

"About thirty seconds before I called you, so," I looked at my phone. "6:02 p.m."

"And you're sure it wasn't here at 5:15?"

"Yep."

"Did you see anyone drive up?"

"Nope, but they could have when I was in the shower and I wouldn't have noticed." Breck nodded, writing in a notebook he pulled out of his back pocket.

"Okay, Lark, I think we are done with you. John, do you know where she's staying tonight?"

"Yep," John answered.

"Good. Thank you for your time. I will see you soon with more questions."

"Great. Mind if I go grab a change of clothing for tonight? *Again.*" I was bitter, really bitter. But life didn't care about my feelings. Or at least this killer didn't. I turned around and went back to my room, grabbing clothing and stuffing them into the same overnight bag I had used yesterday.

I had just finished putting my shirt and toiletries in my bag and was grabbing my underwear when I realized that Cap— *Brecken,* had followed me into my room. Where I was now standing, holding my underwear in front of me, like a flag. *Fudge buckets of biscuits.* We both turned a color red that shouldn't be natural on people.

"I didn't—we needed—you need to be escorted, so I—" He stumbled to a stop, his eyes stuck on the slip of fabric in front of me.

"Yeah. Got it." Why wasn't I moving? Or him? One of us needed to move. Instead he stared at my underwear and I stared at him. Was his gaze heated? It wasn't that surprising that I was attracted to him. If anyone was going to pull my comatose sex drive out of its slumber, it was the man in front of me, but for him to be interested in me? I didn't know what to do.

"They're black." He made that comment and my eyes dropped to my underwear. They were one of my nicer pairs, but not a thong. Some girls swore by them, but unless I was showing, I stayed away from thongs while riding. The main point was they were not my period panties. Or my lounging panties. He wasn't contemplating how big my butt had to be to fit into them. I didn't need to bury myself out back and never be seen again.

But he kept staring.

Was the color important? Was black sexier? What would he say if he noticed they were satin? *Turn around, Lark!*

"Yep." My mind was still screaming, trying to break the moment and get in control of my body, but my hormones had taken over. As long as Brecken stared like that, I wasn't going to move. Instead, I nervously focused on how dry my lips were. As I licked them, his eyes swung up, giving my lips the same focus. I felt my body want to sway toward him, toward the pull of his eyes and the longing I was hoping I wasn't misreading, but fear kept me still. I had only kissed one man in the past ten years. A decade of only one man, touching me, kissing me. What if I did it wrong? What if I read his interest wrong? What if...

"Brecken, do you have a minute? I'm sure that Lark can get her stuff together by herself." John's voice came from the hallway and the moment was broken.

Brecken shook his head, turning a deeper red when he realized he had been staring, and then nodded to me before slipping out. As soon as he had left I sagged to the floor. I hadn't been prepared for what just happened. I wasn't prepared for these... feelings. I brought a hand up to press against my lips. Maybe I might be ready sooner than I thought.

Well, maybe I would wait until sometime after Hailey graduated from high school. That would be soon enough. Once she was taken care of, that was when I could think about these emotions again.

Resolved to ignore my weakness and embarrassment, I went back to packing. Maybe not *those* panties. Grabbing a new pair, one that was substantially less sexy, I went to work. I had everything packed and was zipping up the bag when I realized the black underwear was still sitting on the side of the bag. I hesitated, staring at them. In a moment of weakness, I grabbed the zipper and threw them in, closing the bag before I could change my mind. It was never a bad idea to have another pair, right?

Throwing the bag strap over my shoulder, I headed back to the front porch to check in with the detectives. I wasn't looking forward to lugging it around the bar, but life happened. When I got to the end of the hall, both were leaning over the arm, inspecting the limb from different angles like it might all make sense if they just caught it from the right view. Or they were just looking for evidence. But the second option was less dramatic, so I stuck with my first thought.

"Scrubbed clean again. Just like the leg," John commented quietly to Brecken. I strained to hear them from my hiding place.

"You think they cleaned before or after the amputation? And when's the coroner going to get back to us on his findings?"

"Should be this evening. Maybe tomorrow morning. The county is a little backed up."

"This arm isn't going to give us much more information." He sighed, then looked a little closer. "At least there's a little powder like the last time, maybe from transport? White powder makes me want to guess drugs, but we won't know anything for sure until we get that report. So far, the only lead we have is the drugs. Damn it."

I waited, hoping to overhear more information, but both men went silent, contemplating the arm. 'Possible drugs on the limbs from transport' was all I was getting right then. I could work with that. I thought hard.

Maybe not.

"Okay, I'm off. You guys need anything else? Can I lock up the house?"

"We're good. Go ahead and lock up and I'll catch up with you tomorrow with more questions," Brecken replied with a short nod.

My heart fluttered when he said he would come see me but crashed by the end and I remembered why I didn't date. This attraction thing was annoying. And a serious threat to my cardiac health.

"Yeah, okay, whatever." I slipped around them and headed down the path, closing my eyes at my response. *Whatever?* My inner teen seemed to have come out. I guess that kind of made sense since I met David when I was 20. Maybe my flirting skills just stopped there. *Oh god.* What if I flirted like a teen? How would I even find that out? I couldn't try when I was in town, or Lindsey would write an article about it. This was why I didn't date. Yeah. No dating. Not even detectives with blond hair, blue eyes, and cool shields.

The last one may have been a projection.

CHAPTER 6

Walking from my house, it took about ten minutes to get to The Pub on a normal day. Today it took me five. I wanted to get as far away as possible from the arm, the detective that was driving my hormones crazy, and John, who I suspected enjoyed watching it all happen. The Pub wasn't far enough from my house to satisfy my need to escape, but it had cheap ciders, a huge wine list, and great food. All things that made me happy.

I noticed Jen flirting with a man who I assumed was the new bartender. Then, to my dismay, I got a good look at the town's newest addition. Okay, I had to admit it, she was right. Had I not just been reminded of what a fool I was, I might have been tempted to ignore his age and try my luck anyways. He was over six feet, blond, and had amazing, big blue eyes. Wait... I squinted to get a better look at his face. He had to be wearing eye makeup for them to be that big.

I found a table across the bar. Away from Blue Eyes. And Captain America. And any other man who I didn't have time for or want mucking up my life. What had happened to my little town? Three days ago, Bryan was the hot man in town. Now we had two men that made Bryan look average. *Would have* made Bryan look average. Guilt at my thoughts made me pause. Poor Bryan.

I sat down, throwing my bag under the table, and texted Jen where I was. I may not have wanted any of Blue Eyes, but there was no reason she couldn't try. She wanted a man, even after her cheating ex. Go figure. I guess she was braver than me. I hadn't noticed my surroundings, which was unfortunate when, seconds after I sat down, so did Lindsey.

"Lark! Just the person I wanted to see."

"No comment."

"Oh, please. I'm just here drinking. Like you."

"No comment." But I did give her an 'are you kidding me' look. I had already learned my lesson with Lindsey.

"Off the record, Lark." She held up both hands. "I promise." I studied her face to try and tell if she was being truthful. Hmm...

"No comment."

"Oh, please. Like you know anything I don't. You didn't send yourself body parts, and there's nothing about you that's interesting enough to warrant threatening."

"Someone disagrees," I shot back, then mentally kicked myself. Why was I arguing this? Had I really just gotten upset about Lindsey saying that I wasn't interesting enough to threaten? She got under my skin too easily.

"Really? Why do you think that?"

That earned her another look. I knew what she was doing.

"No comment."

"So, the police think that someone is threatening you with body parts. Interesting, interesting. You didn't have much of a relationship with Bryan. I mean, everyone knew he asked you out, but you turned him down. Just like you turned down every other eligible male in this town."

"I've only been asked out by two men since I moved here a year ago. That can't be every eligible male in this town." Then I thought about it.

She may have a point.

"Either way, you don't date. You don't stay out late or party. All you do is raise your child and ride your horses. It's boring."

"It's called being an adult. You might want to try it."

"Please." She waved her hand dismissively. I felt an overwhelming urge to bite it when it came too close to my face, but that would have undermined my adult argument. "I make more than most of the people in this town through the advertising on my blogs. I adult just fine."

The grammar police would disagree.

"That's nice." I had already learned not to ask Lindsey about her blogs. Any of them. Everyone made that mistake once, but only the most desperate guys did it twice. It may be unkind of me, but there was a reason why someone as pretty as her was still single.

"As one of the few other female business

entrepreneurs in this town, you have to know how it intimidates men." Lindsey preened a little as she pointed out her success.

Good, then they stayed away. But it didn't seem to be intimidating Captain America. Or the butthead who kept leaving me body parts.

"I can't say I've noticed." I scanned the room, looking for an escape. Where was the waitress? Or Jen? The bartender couldn't be that cute. I looked again. Maybe he was. I would not be getting Jen's attention anytime soon.

"That's the only reason I'm still single. Men can't handle it when they find out I make more than them."

Okay, in my experience that was also true, but it was likely not the only reason.

"Did you ever date Bryan?" I asked. Now that I thought about it, it was weird I hadn't heard any rumors about the two of them. Lindsey's name had been linked to most of the single men in this town at one point or another. And some of the married ones as well.

"Please. We went to school together before his family moved to be closer to his mother's sister." She got my full attention again.

"Really? I thought he was a transplant like me."

"Nope. Born and raised, mostly. He left senior year and came back when he was—" She squinted trying to remember. "Twenty-five? Wait, I was just getting my blog going after the newspaper closed, so more like twenty-four. Right after he got out of the Marines."

"So, you grew up with him?" I asked.

"Yep. His family lived down the street from me."

"What was he like in high school?"

"A cheater. He cheated on girls, at school, and in life. A loser, through and through."

"So super popular." I knew the type.

"You got it."

"Huh. Was he dating anyone recently?"

"Yep. I would guess multiple people, but the only one I saw was that girl from the resort. The night manager."

"The resort?" This was getting good.

"Yes. I know her from the last time Laura came to talk to me about advertising. Laura brought her along. Anyway, I saw them out on a date last week. All hot and heavy. Posted a picture on my blog, even. They were out in Misne. You know, the small town in the mountains? They probably didn't want anyone knowing about them, but I saw them anyway."

"What were you doing in Misne?" I figured asking more questions might keep her talking.

"That's where I meet up with my programmer for my website. She won't drive all the way out here, but she loves Misne." Lindsey sniffed at the thought anyone could like another town over Barrow Bay. She may have many, many faults, but she was loyal to the town.

"Interesting. I wonder if she knew his reputation." I certainly hadn't. Then again, I wasn't interested to begin with, so it wasn't information I cared about.

"Probably not. He didn't date a lot within the town once he came back," she told me. "And most people excuse behavior like that in high school."

"You don't?"

"Nope. Once a cheater, always a cheater."

"Here, here." We clinked our glasses. Well, she clinked her glass. I stole a used one that hadn't been cleared from the table.

"Not that any man would cheat on all this." She gestured to her body, which was amazing, showcased in a tiny black dress that pushed her boobs almost to her chin. I sighed internally.

"Can I get you anything?" Josie, the waitress, interrupted us. Her curly hair bounced back and forth with the speed of her stop. Thank the pizza gods. Escape!

"Can I have a pineapple cider and a pepperoni pizza?" It had been a hard day. I deserved it.

"That's it?" she asked, eyeing Lindsey. They also went to school together, and I remembered rumors of some bad blood between them. Supposedly, Josie accused Lindsey of trying to move in on her man. Lindsey hadn't denied it.

"I'm out of here. The atmosphere doesn't seem to agree with me anymore." Lindsey got up with a sniff and downed the rest of her drink before walking towards the door.

"Was she bothering you, Lark?" Josie asked as we watched Lindsey 'accidentally' bump into the new bartender as he was coming out from behind the bar to help a waitress, earning her a glare from Jen and a long boob glance from the new guy. To my jaded eye, the glance looked less admiring and more reproachful about how much boob was showing. But my man-reading skills sucked. With a shake of my head I turned back to Josie.

"She was surprisingly civil for someone who is making money off my misfortune," I said, smiling at her.

"Yeah, we all read about your body parts issue. Do they know who it is and why they keep landing on your door?"

"Nope. No comment." I winked to take the sting out of my refusal. Let her think I was joking about Lindsey.

"Hah. Not giving up any of your secrets, huh? That had to drive Lindsey mad."

"She took it okay. She was the one telling me about her high school." Josie gave me a surprised look before it turned thoughtful.

"That's right. We all went to school together. Wow, I had forgotten about Bryan until now. He left before Senior year."

"Lindsey told me he was super popular."

"He would have been prom king if they had let us have a junior prom. He was the big man on campus."

"And dated a lot of girls?" I prompted.

"God yes. I'll never forget the fight in the cafeteria. Who was it, again? Wait! I think it was between Laura and Lindsey! What a small world. I only remember because the names were so similar. One of the guys even made a rhyme out of it. Laura must have loved having him crawl back and ask her for a job. Wow. That seems like a lifetime ago."

"I know what you mean," I murmured, hoping she might go on, but she didn't.

"Well, I got to get back to work. It's slammed tonight."

"Yeah, I noticed you seem a little busy," I commented. She looked at me and then after glancing around to see who was looking, slipped into the chair beside me.

Leaning in close, she asked, "You know Becky, right?" She waited for my nod before continuing with a glare in Lindsey's direction. Lindsey was still flirting with Blue Eyes and Jen's body was rigid with rage. "She took tonight off. She was dating Bryan and just couldn't stop crying about everything."

"Becky was dating Bryan?" I whispered back.

"Yeppers. For five months now. He wanted her to keep it quiet, but you know Becky. She couldn't keep a secret if the President himself came down and asked her to."

"Wow. Poor Becky." Lucky Bryan. Two girls at the same time? And I couldn't even talk to one ridiculously handsome man. *Dang.*

"I know, right? Don't tell Lindsey. We're trying to keep Becky's name out of her clutches."

"As Lindsey's latest victim, I know how you feel." She smiled at my sarcasm and got up to go put my order in.

"I'll be back with your drink. Food shouldn't take long. We started the pizza when we saw you come in."

"I love you. Divorce your husband and marry me."

"Ahh, honey, you don't make enough for me." She winked at me before sashaying away. It was sad I was so predictable. I also needed to start eating healthier. More salads, maybe some fish. I'd start another day.

Jen finally sauntered over, a frown on her face and

two drinks in her hand.

"I hate Lindsey."

"That's a pretty big club."

"Stupid double-D's." She looked down at her boobs and fluffed them. "When did a C cup become deficient?"

"Coming from someone who only got boobs after pregnancy, I have no idea."

"Yeah, but you have the whole 'skinny waif' thing going for you. You could be a model. The rest of us have to work for it."

"I work out for a living," I pointed out with a glare. I did not look like a waif. She just ignored me in favor of complaining about her body.

"I sit all day and my butt shows it. Maybe I could put the bike pedals under my desk? That way I could work and workout at the same time?"

"Will you be stable enough to work without falling out of the chair?"

She thought about it. "Probably not." She finished her drink in one gulp and slammed it down. "I made a decision."

"Okay."

But instead of continuing, she took a deep breath, then deflated and grabbed the other drink. This must be big news.

"I'm going to try online dating," she announced.

I stared. "That's it?"

"What do you mean? That's huge! It's online dating! With men. Outside of Barrow Bay!" she cried.

"Well, I would assume so since there are only three hot guys." I winced. "Two hot guys." We both sobered slightly at the reminder.

"Poor Bryan."

"You know, other than Becky and Laura, no one else seems to be taking his death very hard," I commented. Then I felt bad. I had missed his presence at the coffee shop but I wasn't mourning him at all. Other than to wish his body parts would stop showing up at my house. I was really a horrible person. But his body parts now stood between me and my daughter. Wait. The leg wasn't standing. Sat? Laid? Unimportant. The point was that I wanted my daughter back. Immediately.

"Well, what do you expect? He was a bad influence in these parts." Joe, the owner, commented as he slid into the bench beside Jen. She nodded at him but went back to contemplating her drink. "What's her deal?" he asked me. Jen pretended to ignore him. Or maybe actually was, as she didn't even blink at his comment.

"Lindsey stole the new bartender." Joe doubled over in laughter, slapping his knee a few times. I lifted an eyebrow at him. "Well, that's not the reaction I was expecting."

"Will? Tall, dark and as gay as Rupert Everett, over there?" He pointed at the new bartender. Jen finally gave us her full attention.

"He's gay?" she exclaimed.

"And married. His husband is amazing. A bigwig in the Drag Queen scene in San Fran."

"No." She elongated the word in her shock.

"Yes."

"Hah!" They both looked at me. "I guessed that he

was wearing eyeliner when I came in."

"That's making assumptions based on stereotypes," Jen said primly.

"He is, isn't he?" I couldn't hold back my smirk.

"No!" That was too much emphasis. I pinned her with a stare. "Okay, he is, but I didn't want to judge! Straight men are starting to wear it, too!" she protested, as I shook my head at her.

"So how long do you think it takes for Lindsey to catch on?" I asked. We all looked over at the seat Lindsey was parked in at the bar, her boobs dangerously high and multiple drinks in front of her.

"Hopefully a few weeks. I could use some of that blog money," Joe said with a smile. "Here's your food." He got up as Josie put the pizza down.

"Pizza and pineapple cider? Could you be any more boring?" Jen demanded.

"Hey! Pineapple cider is different! Most people get pear or apple," I defended myself, as I lifted a piece of pizza.

"You keep thinking that."

"I will. Today has sucked, but pizza makes it better."

"Don't worry. Tomorrow has to get better."

I had a sinking feeling in my gut. I was pretty sure that was the same phrase I told myself before falling asleep last night.

CHAPTER 7

I was right. It didn't get better.

And not just because of the painting, which I had decided needed to be destroyed in a tragic bonfire while I made s'mores and sang whatever campfire songs I could remember. No, the painting was just the start.

There was still no coffee.

"How can you live like this?!" I wanted to yell it at Jen but yelling required energy and energy required coffee, and, well, no coffee.

"Not everyone is caffeine dependent!" Jen growled back at me.

"But you went to the store. You got food. How did you not get coffee?"

"I forgot! It isn't something I normally need. I didn't see you remembering to bring any."

She had a point.

"How are you energetic this early in the morning without coffee?" I asked, before my head hit the table. The lovely scrambled eggs and toast that Jen had made me sat next to my head, uneaten. There was no eating before coffee. I heard her sigh in disgust at my theatrics, and I knew there was an eye-roll or two thrown in for good measure. Jen was an eye-roller.

"You may want to complain less and eat more."

"Why?" I asked, without taking my head off the table.

"It's Thursday."

"So?"

"It's *Thursday*." Finally, her emphasis got through to my tired brain. *Oh no.* I lifted my head and shoveled in food.

Today was the Whale Watch. It was a tourist attraction that the local fisherman started years ago. The first time Liam had rented out his boat to some tourists, his plan was to take them out, see some birds, maybe a dolphin or two, and come back saying they 'just missed' the whales. Instead, they found a whole pod that breached right next to the boat. One video, ten days, and thousands of followers later, Liam now had a thriving business he ran one day a week. He said he only ran it one day because he didn't want to give up his true love: fishing. The locals all knew it was because that first trip was a fluke. We never see whales. Liam's trips come back with a ten percent rate of finding anything whale-like. But the tourists still paid just in case they might be the next lucky sucker to almost die from a capsized boat in a whale pod.

All of this meant that the coffee shop was overrun every Thursday from 6-8 a.m. when Liam left for his cruise. And with no Bryan? It would be total chaos. No food. Drinks that took forever. It was enough to make me debate how much I needed coffee. Not enough to give up, but enough to debate.

"Do you think Tops will still have coffee?" I asked through mouthfuls. We didn't have time for me to wait to swallow. Swallowing was for beginners. "Whoever killed Bryan is seriously pissing me off." I forced the words out between bites.

"You weren't pissed off before? I would have been pissed since the first body part."

"It's a sliding scale. Leg, mild torture. Arm, murder. Forcing me to deal with Whale-Watching Thursday with them down their best barista? Now I'm starting to understand why anyone would go through the effort of dismemberment."

"Oh, please. You're too lazy even with coffee to dismember someone."

I looked at her, and that comment shook a thought loose in my brain.

"Dismemberment is hard."

"Um, yes?"

"Like really hard, right?"

"I mean, I haven't actually looked into it since, you know, I don't murder people, but I would assume so." She eyed me.

"And bloody."

"Okay. I'm getting you coffee today. This," she gestured at me, "is starting to scare me."

"No, no. I mean, yes, but no, follow the thought. You would need a big room to dismember a body, preferably one that's easy to clean. And a big tool. Is a woman even strong enough to do it?"

"Thanks for putting women's rights back twenty

years, and yes. We have tools for that."

"Don't think I didn't notice how quickly you had that answer." I lifted my eyebrows in challenge, and she sighed before giving me an answer.

"Chainsaw. A woman can use a chainsaw."

"Have you used a chainsaw?" She was giving females credit I didn't deserve. Last time I tried to use a chainsaw, it won.

"No, but how hard could it be?"

"Hard."

"Don't think we won't be circling back to how you know that. But, if I'm following your logic, you think that the killer is a man. One with access to a chainsaw?"

"Or axe." I held up my phone, which I had grabbed while we talked. "It says here that an axe is actually less messy and only slightly harder to use."

"What are you looking at? Is the page www dot serial killer dot com? Is this something people normally look up? Like someone wakes up and thinks, 'It's a beautiful day. I wonder, how could I dismember a body?'"

"Okay, one— mystery writers do that," I said. "And two— the person who answered is a butcher. He cuts up full animals on a regular basis."

"I really need to become a vegetarian. That's disgusting."

I looked up from my phone and stared at her. "You are currently eating eggs."

"Vegetarians eat eggs!"

"No. I mean that we are eating breakfast while trying to figure out how to dismember a human body, and what bothers you is that a butcher is the one that answered."

"Are you telling me it doesn't bother you that this man cuts animals up for a living and is promoting himself as a dismemberment expert online?"

"He's just trying to be helpful," I defended him.

"Helpful about cutting up bodies!"

"He's not..." I had nothing. "Okay, it's a little creepy. But he has good information."

"This is how it all starts. Today, you're just looking. Finding out how the 'cool kids' cut up their corpses. Next thing you know, you're out of control. Just jonesing until you get your next fix."

"You are insane in the morning," I told her. "You know that, right?"

"An ex or two might have mentioned it."

"It's the no-coffee thing. It leaves you unstable," I muttered under my breath.

"Give it up on the no-coffee thing! Not. Everyone. Drinks. Coffee!"

We sat there in silence for a second, the only noise the sound of our forks on the plate.

"Does anyone even say 'jonesing' anymore?"

"Shut up, coffee bitch."

"Jeez. You are mean in the morning."

"Don't you have a coffee shop to conquer? Go away." My plate disappeared into the sink as she glared at me.

Wow. I couldn't remember the last time I got a home-cooked meal and didn't have to do the dishes. It was kind of nice. I sat back in my seat to enjoy it.

"Lark?"

"Yes?"

"Thursday!"

"Shiitake mushrooms!" I grabbed my purse and ran out the door. But before it shut behind me, I turned and poked my head back in.

"And just so you know, nothing is disturbing enough for me to give up bacon!" Then I slammed the door and took off at what I claimed was a brisk walk. It was the gait in between a light jog and running for my life. I would have thought that in the last thirty years I had matured enough to let someone else have the last word. But I was wrong.

I walked the two blocks to Tops quickly, but I was still disappointed at the length of the line when I got there. It was out the door, five people waiting just to get inside. I slipped into the line behind a couple from the L.A. area who were elated about their fun day on the water. They just knew they were going to get some great pictures of whales. *Good luck.*

Behind me a younger man, maybe eighteen-years-old, stepped into line. The boy was grungy, his clothing stained and wrinkled, his hair so oily I was surprised none dripped off. I expected a smell to emanate from him, but surprisingly he smelled freshly cleaned. Maybe this was the desired result? Or was he just that lazy? It was a toss-up. I tried to be the better person and not give into my instinct to move away from him, but I found myself edging closer to the couple anyway. He was shifting his weight and glancing around almost constantly. Actions I used to reason with myself when I gave in and moved away from him. He was the definition of shifty.

"Larklyn! My light! What are you doing here this morning?"

Oh no.

"Hey, Gran. How are you this morning?"

"Fine. Fine. Larklyn, it's Thursday. Why are you here? You should be home."

"I don't want to talk about it."

"That's okay. You can tell me about it when you come over tonight."

Oh no. Really, no. "I'm sorry Gran, but—"

"You want to bring something! No, I won't hear of it. Bring food to a dinner at my house? Unacceptable! Rude! Implying I can't feed you. You know better, Larklyn."

Dagnabit. She purposely misunderstood me. I was in trouble. Maybe Jen could come and buffer me. "Okay, Gran, I'll be there at seven."

"Six is perfect, Larklyn. Thank you for suggesting it."

Yep. I was in big trouble.

"See you then," I said with a weak smile and an even weaker wave.

"Until then! Love you." Gran walked away and I let out a sigh only to realize that Shifty had jumped the line to stand in front of me. I thought about saying something, but I could put more distance between us when he was in front, so I let it go.

It took me ten minutes to get to the front of the

line, keeping a decent distance from Shifty. I noticed the couple that had been in front of me eyeing him as well and felt a little better. I might have been judging him, but at least I wasn't the only one.

As we got closer to the front of the line, he got more and more agitated, running his hand through his hair and glancing around to catch glimpses out the door. I was contemplating the likelihood that the store was about to be robbed when Laura greeted him. Trying to hide my paranoia, I looked out the window as I watched out the corner of my eye.

"Hello. May I take your order?" Laura greeted him with a frazzled smile.

"I have a package for Bryan."

Laura stopped what she was doing and looked at him.

"You can't deliver it here. What is Fee thinking?" she hissed, looking around. I caught her eye, and she froze for a second, judging the distance between us before changing her tune. "Bryan is dead. If you have anything for him, you need to take it to the police."

"Listen, lady. I don't care who takes it, but I need to be paid."

"I can't help you," Laura said firmly. "Do you want anything to drink? Maybe on the house for your inconvenience?" She gave him a customer service smile, one that reached from ear to ear but missed her eyes, and held a cup up as if to tempt him.

"Fine. Mocha. *If* it's on the house."

"Completely on me." Her smile tightened until it was more a grimace than anything else as she watched him walk away. She finished with his order and I stopped pretending that I was people-watching.

"Hey, Lark. Your usual?" Laura greeted me.

"Please."

"No problem." She rang up my order, but as she handed me back my change, I couldn't help myself.

"Who was that? The guy in front of me?"

"One of Bryan's friends from the city. No one important. Forget about him." Laura overplayed her dismissiveness, her hands too emphatic as they waved him away. I was pretty sure she was lying to me.

"One of Bryan's friends from the city?"

"Yes."

She moved on to the next customer, and the wait in line gave me more time to analyze the 'friend' who was now with me in the group waiting for our drinks. Disregarding his lack of concern over Bryan's demise, I was still struggling to believe this man had the financial means to drive three hours on a Thursday morning to a small town whose only claim to fame was one resort. From the condition of his shoes, I was surprised that he had a car at all. The shoes were beyond dirty, their days of being white faded into a brown that varied by location. The sole on the right shoe was splitting away, and his sock peeked through. It didn't matter how lazy he was. If he had the money, those shoes would have been a goner.

I looked back at Laura, who was glancing over at us with greater frequency than the crowd should allow. She had a frown on her face every time her head swung around to locate the boy and then slipped to me. I tried to look less interested than I was, but I continued to be on her radar until my drink came up, jumping over several people who had been there before me. I think Laura wanted to get me out of the shop as quickly as possible. I took my coffee with a smile, but I couldn't help one last look at both Laura and Shifty as I walked out the door. Laura was whispering to him as she handed him the cup of coffee and a paper. I was pretty sure she wasn't giving him her number.

I kept my head down as I walked back to my truck, which was still parked at my house. When did Laura start knowing Bryan's friends? From what I knew, they had a professional relationship, but she seemed more... invested in the package Shifty was delivering than she should have been. And what fee was she talking about? As I reached my truck, I tucked those thoughts away. Bryan's death needed to be solved so my daughter could come home, but I needed to make money first.

CHAPTER 8

Around midday I got a text from John releasing my house.

Again.

At least the team collecting evidence was getting quicker at getting my porch back to me. I just hoped this was the last time. After texting Jen to let her know I was hopefully back in my own house tonight, I went back to letting the smell of horses and my connection to these amazing animals drive away my issues at home. This was my happy place. On the back of an animal that couldn't talk but still be perfectly in sync with me, moving together as one. It was magic.

I bit the bullet and called my ex during my lunch break to tell him the cliff notes version of my recent deliveries, and he agreed to let Hailey stay one more week. She sounded excited about it. There was some big festival in one of the towns near them and she wanted to go, so the timing was perfect. I got body parts, and she got a festival. Being an adult was not fair.

I was getting off of Buddy, my lesson master, when the mailman pulled up. George McCullens was a man in his mid-fifties who personified the image of a mailman and did it with pride. He had silver-grey hair that had gone grey in his twenties and was receding back from his forehead at the corners of his face. Combined with a friendly smile and a penchant for corny jokes, he made friends wherever he went. He was so popular that no one had the heart to tell him his failing eyesight was a problem. George was so proud that he had gotten to this age without 'enhancements,' as he referred to what the rest of us called 'glasses.' Either way, reading was becoming harder for him and misdeliveries were becoming more common. He also liked to deliver the mail in person, a quirk I had learned to deal with.

"Lark! I just knew you would be here."

I managed to keep my smile instead of asking him where else I would be at three in the afternoon. George didn't get sarcasm. Or negativity of any sort. When I first met him, I thought no one could really be that nice. He had to be fake. Now I knew better. He was as real as a pie for the Sewing Circle. Sure, some of the ladies might fudge a little and use corn syrup instead of pure, organic cane sugar, but really, who was complaining about that?

"You couldn't deliver to the house the last few days, huh?" I prompted, curious what he might have that was worth driving out here to deliver.

"Yeah, when I saw all the police tape, I decided to just deliver the past few days' mail to you out here. That way I could check in on you and make sure you're okay." He had gotten out of his truck, a big package in his hands that he put down on the mounting block outside the barn. "How are you doing, sweetie? I know that getting all those body parts couldn't be easy. Do they have any leads? Do they know why you keep getting them?"

"Not that they're willing to tell me. Evidently, getting body parts doesn't give me any more gossip than not getting them. Go figure."

"I'm sorry, sweetie. It'll be all over soon. John'll catch them. Don't you worry none."

"I won't, George. Thanks for dropping this off."

"No problem, no problem at all."

I waited until he pulled out of the parking lot and turned back down the road before I looked at the package. *Fudge buckets.*

Annie Phan. Again. One of these days I would remember to read the name on the package before George leaves me with someone else's mail.

Annie Phan was a Vietnamese woman in her late sixties that had moved to the town some time ago. Her black hair, streaked with just a hint of gray, was worn short in a fashionable bob around her face and set off her deep-set smile lines and glimmering eyes in a way that always made me smile whenever I saw her. Which was starting to be every week.

Luckily for me, she seemed to have quasi-adopted me after I dropped off her package the second time, and she was a fantastic cook. I had a weakness for pho soup that was unfulfilled on the old-fashioned streets of Barrow Bay. I had started calling Annie my pho dealer. She just smiled and said that she loved to feed people. Her two sons both lived in the Bay area, although they came out frequently to see her, and the whole family had come to be an adorable addition to the town.

Unfortunately for me, whoever sent her packages thought we lived on the same street. I lived on Old Cottage Road. Annie lived on Old Cottage Street. After cursing the Mayor who didn't want to use more diverse street names and George's failing eyesight, I gave in to the inevitable and decided to trade pho for package delivery.

I picked up the package and put it in my truck passenger seat so that I could drop it off on my way home and went back to untacking my horse after sending Annie a text to let her know I would be coming after work. I was washing my last horse off when a newer car pulled in and parked next to my truck. It took me a moment to remember whose car it was, but when I did, I focused back on my task. If I let myself watch him approach, I was going to have trouble talking. Again.

"Hello, Larklyn." Captain's voice came from behind me, and I took a deep breath to prepare myself for the sight.

"Please. Just Lark." I turned around and there he was. The same blond movie star look-alike from last night. Without his sidekick. "Where's John?"

"He had other things to do today, and I had more questions for you."

I used the excuse of putting away my grooming supplies to think about his answer. Something about it wasn't right.

"You have questions and he doesn't agree," I threw out, and when he blushed, I knew I had hit it on the head. "Sorry, Detective. I have plans today. Can't answer questions just to satisfy your paranoia." I moved past him to take the horse back to her stall, and he followed.

"What plans?" I stopped and turned to look at him, my eyebrows meeting my hairline at his tone.

"I'm sorry. Is there a rule against having a life when people are terrorizing you with body parts?" I snapped.

"Not if you are following the law, but if you aren't, I'm going to find out." It came out suspicious and over-the-top, and even he seemed to notice. His face flushed slightly more before he lifted his chin. I guess he was sticking to his guns.

"You realize you sound like a B-movie villain right now."

"It takes one to know one." He gave me a smirk.

"Wow." I blinked a few times trying to absorb that answer. I turned and walked the last few feet to the horse's stall and let her free before turning back to him. "I can't remember what my comeback to that was in *middle school*, but I know I used to have a whopper."

"I try to exceed expectations." He shrugged with one shoulder, shaking off the absurdity of our conversation with a slight smile he tried to suppress. I was pretty sure I was amusing the hardened, suspicious detective despite himself.

"What are your questions?" I checked my phone. Almost five o'clock and Annie's house was only ten minutes away. I had time to swing by and drop off the package before heading to my house to get changed on my way to Gran's. If I didn't get stuck answering questions with the detective.

"Where were you Monday?"

"I already told John. We went through my whole

day in detail. Go get it from him."

"Why are you refusing to answer?"

"Honestly? Because that was days ago, and I don't remember."

"Can you try?"

"I dropped Hailey off at her father's in the morning. I got an unremarkable lunch on the way back. I can check my accounts to get you the name of the restaurant. Came home. Cleaned house. Binge-watched any TV show I could find that isn't appropriate for a seven-year-old. You know, generally went wild."

"You didn't mention dinner," he commented as he wrote everything down.

"Really?" He looked up at my question and nodded. Great. "Wine and peanut M&Ms."

"Peanut M&M's? For dinner?" He glanced up at me, a little judgy.

"I do a healthy breakfast, lunch and dinner every day Hailey is here," I justified. "When she's gone, I tend to overdo it the other way. It's all about balance, right?"

"I'm pretty sure that isn't what they mean."

It was my turn to shrug. I checked my phone again and then grabbed my keys. "I have to go. Can we do this tomorrow?"

"I'm afraid not. We need to do it now."

"Well, unless you want to ride with me and continue your questioning on the way, that isn't going to work."

"Okay."

Fiddlesticks. Should have seen that one coming.

"Okay what?" Please don't say you are coming.

"Okay. I will ride with you to your plans."

"You want to come with me?" Shock was starting to lose out to glee. I could make this work for me. Captain at one of Gran's dinners? The day was starting to look up.

No. I wasn't that evil.

"No, but I would like to see what these *plans* are." He gave me a flat look.

And look at that. I *was* that evil.

"Well, okay then. I hope you're hungry because there will be a lot of food coming your way."

I watched his brow lower as he thought about how food played into my nefarious plans. I even let myself smile at him as I picked up the last of my things and walked to the truck, me leading with renewed energy and him trailing with clear hesitation. I swung around to grab the package and throw it in the back seat, before going to the driver's side door.

"You absolutely sure about this?" I asked. One more chance to run.

"Yes." But his narrow eyes said not really. I chuckled and got into the truck, hoisting myself into the seat and shoving the keys in the ignition as he rushed to make sure I didn't escape.

"You going to tell me where we're going now?"

"Annie's."

"I don't remember that being on the tour John gave me."

"It wasn't." I pulled the truck out of the driveway and pulled onto the road heading in the opposite direction of my house, and Captain started to shift his weight. I watched him out of the corner of my eye, enjoying his nerves before I gave him one more out. "You can still back out. I can turn around and drop you off."

"That implies that there's a point in which you can't turn around and drop me off." He replied, glancing at me with his lips pressed into a line.

"Yep." I kept it simple; I was having too much fun being the cause of the discomfort instead of the victim. "So, are you going to ask those questions?"

"Why do you think that you keep getting body parts?"

I turned on my blinker and turned left into Annie's housing community while I thought about my answer. It didn't help.

"I have no idea. Lindsey is right. I'm boring. I have very little in terms of a social life, and what I have revolves around Jen and my family. I don't go out very often and when I do, I'm home before ten because I have to be at work by eight, if not earlier. Nothing body-worthy."

"Your business isn't doing very well."

Ouch.

"I cover my bills. That's about all you can really expect from a training business."

"But you own the stable, too," he pointed out.

"Okay, that's about all you can expect from a horse business. Especially one out here where there are so few residents to pull potential clients from."

"Have you thought about other avenues to make

money?"

"Avenues to make money?" What, like drugs?

"Yep."

"Nope."

"Really?" He turned to look me straight in the eye and his brow furrowed further. "I don't know anyone who makes as little as you do who doesn't think about making more money. You don't have any spousal support. How are you supporting yourself and your daughter?"

How did he know how little I made and yet not know about my inheritance?

"We do fine. Don't need more money."

"Horses are expensive. Kids are expensive. You have an expensive life."

"You're telling me," I muttered as I made a right. Two more turns and I could drop off the package.

"Where are we going?" He looked around at the houses before turning back to me. "This is a residential road."

"1124 Old Cottage Street." Another right and I slowed down as we approached Annie's house.

"This isn't your street. And I thought we were going to Annie's, whatever that is."

I pulled off to the side of the road and parked, turning off the car. Grabbing the package and my purse, I opened the door and got out. Captain just waited in the seat, watching me.

"Are you staying in the truck? Because there will be pho involved and it might take a little while. Your choice." He got out of the truck slowly, glancing around at the neighborhood before assessing the house.

Annie's home was in a new development that they had made in the 'old' style. Cottage chic. Urban lines with cottage details was what it felt like to me, but they sold quickly and well, so maybe I was alone in my dislike of the facade. The front lawn was neat and well-tended, the grass cut to a good length. She kept the corners sharp without any encroaching weeds like I always found in mine. I knew the backyard was elaborate and beautiful from past visits.

Annie was the kind of gardener I wished I could be. Or, at least pay for. She was always finding new ways to combine the natural flora and plants from Vietnam into a soothing hide-away, complete with a table that we'd had tea on. She always made me feel inadequate. She could cook and garden like a professional, she had impeccable style, and she did it all while raising her children. I managed to get myself dressed and convince thousand-pound animals not to mess with me. It wasn't quite the same.

"How, in a town this small, do you have two streets with the same name?"

"We don't. I live on Old Cottage Road. This is Old Cottage *Street*."

"It's almost the same."

"Yep, the old mayor wanted a theme, but ran out of names. Then started to reuse the old ones with a different street type. We voted him out soon after. Not soon enough to stop this one, though, which is why Annie keeps having packages delivered to me. Most of the professionals and locals know the difference, but

George, our mailman, well, he won't admit he needs glasses."

"So, instead of pointing out the issue, you just deliver it for him?"

"Well, she bribes me with soup. What's a girl to do?" I asked, before turning and knocking. I heard scurrying and someone yelling inside, but I couldn't make out the words. It only took a few seconds before the door opened and Annie was there to greet us. When she saw me, a smile transformed her face, and she hugged me.

"Lark! How are you? We have been following your trouble. You poor thing." She ended the hug by grabbing my hands and patting them. I returned her fond smile.

"You must be Annie," Captain interrupted, and we both turned to him, me with my eyes trying to communicate to 'be nice' and Annie with surprise.

"Lark, you brought a man with you." She smiled at me, her eyes sparkling in delight at this new turn of events. I guess she was on the 'Lark needs a boyfriend' train, too.

"He insisted that he needed to question me and wouldn't take no for an answer," I joked. Her reaction was sudden and abrupt.

"He's a cop." Before the words were even out of her mouth, the door was shut and there was screaming on the other side. My jaw dropped at the change and I stared at the closed door, package in hand, for a few seconds before turning to Captain.

"Well. Do you always get such a reaction wherever you go?"

"No. Not really. Usually people like me. Just the people in this town have been difficult."

I frowned. I was pretty sure he was including me in the 'people.'

"Well, she liked me just fine until you showed up. Usually I would have a bowl of soup and cookies to go by now. Now I'm standing out here, like an idiot, not knowing what to do." I turned back to the door and knocked again. "Annie? I still have your package. Do you want me to just leave it out here?" I called through the door, and I heard more movement inside the house, but no answer. I waited one more second before putting the package down on the front step and taking off for the truck, sending glares at Captain every so often.

When we were in the truck and I was turning it on, I couldn't hold myself back anymore.

"You cost me pho," I said, my eyes narrowing to pin him down. He ignored me. In fact, now that I realized it, he had been ignoring my irritation since Annie slammed the door in my face. That was not going to work for me. "HELLO!"

He jumped and his eyes finally focused on me.

"How often do the packages get misdelivered?"

"Nope. We are going to deal with the important part first. YOU COST ME PHO!"

"Whatever. I will buy you some at another time—"

"That would be great, but short of us going into San Francisco, there is no other place to get pho. Just Annie. You cost me my dealer…" Oh.

Oh no.

No, no, no, no.

He watched my face, taking in the emotions that I'm sure were evident. Once he seemed to think I was done, he asked his question again.

"How often do you get packages for Annie?"

"It was once a month, but recently it has been every week."

"On the same day?"

I thought back. "Yes."

"What is Annie's last name?"

"Phan." His face went white and then completely blank. Well, this just kept getting better and better.

"And her family?"

"Her husband is dead. She has two sons."

"Their names?"

"Henry and Andrew." His lips tightened when I said their names and I knew I was right.

Annie Phan, sweet little Annie Phan, was a drug dealer.

CHAPTER 9

I need to go back to my car." Captain pulled out his phone and texted someone, his fingers flying over the screen as he worked on this new break in the case. I checked the time and sighed. 5:45 p.m. I had two choices: make the detective happy and my grandmother unhappy or make my grandmother happy and the detective—who would leave for San Francisco at the end of this case—unhappy. So many choices.

"Sorry. You remember when I told you there was a point of no return? We reached it about five minutes ago. You can just come with me."

"No. I need to go." He didn't even look up at me when he made his demand, and just expected me to follow his orders. This man needed more people in his life who didn't jump to do his bidding.

"Ask John to come pick you up. He'll know where you'll be." That got him to put his phone down and look at me.

"This is one of those small-town things, isn't it?"

"More like a grandmother thing. She called a family dinner tonight at six sharp."

His face turned into a glare.

"You couldn't have just told me that your plans were a family dinner?"

"Would you have believed me?" He opened his mouth and then closed it again with a click. His follow-up glare told me I was right. He wouldn't have.

I pulled out of the complex going as fast as I felt comfortable with since there was a cop in my car, which meant the speed limit. Exactly. Glancing over, trying to decide how much I could push it, I noticed him typing into his phone and ignoring me. Deciding to risk it, I pressed down on the gas and brought my speed up, glancing at him every so often. He seemed engrossed, and I relaxed and let myself drive a little faster.

"I think five above the speed limit is enough, don't you, Larklyn?"

"Can you please stop calling me Larklyn? Only my Gran uses that name." I looked down at the speedometer and then back at Captain. "How did you do that?"

"Know how fast you're going? It's magic."

Right.

"Training," I guessed. His head bob and corresponding smirk told me I was right again.

"That's a kind of magic." He even lifted his head so I could see his face, before frowning at the phone again. "John can't pick me up until eight. He says he's busy. What could he be doing?"

"Avoiding you," I teased before grinning and answering the question. "And driving his wife to the store. Tomorrow is the Sewing Circle, and she's hosting it. As I heard it, Sally Mae was telling Judy—"

"Someone's name is Sally Mae?" he asked, and I was

rewarded with another glance. A judgmental one, but a glance. I was starting to enjoy seeing how often I could distract him from his phone.

"It's a fine name, Brecken. You need to be less judgmental."

"How old is Sally Mae, exactly?"

Eighty. But that didn't fit well with my 'be less judgmental' argument.

"Over fifty."

"Really?" He pinned me with his eyes as if he knew I was hedging the truth.

"Okay. She turned eighty this year. But she could be younger!"

"No, she couldn't," he muttered.

"Do you want the rest of the story or not?" I demanded.

"Not really, no."

"Fine."

"Fine."

Yep. Just a couple of adults over here.

We sat in silence for the rest of the ride, him busy with his phone and me sulking about his lack of sulking. We pulled up at Gran's house at 5:58 p.m. and I jumped out of the truck, just barely turning it off and pulling the keys out as my cousin Janet ran up on foot. I left the detective to make his own way in as we both rushed to be at the door by six. She cleared a small hedge as she ran over the lawn to get to the door, and I cut corners off the walkway as I checked my phone. 5:59 p.m.

Janet and I reached the door, bouncing into each other as we came to an abrupt stop. We made it. One minute to spare. I knocked while we both listened for the grandfather clock to signal the hour.

Bong. Bong. Bong.

Gran opened the door, pinning both of us with a look as the clock continued to chime.

Bong. Bong. Bong.

She waited until the last sound had stopped before she opened her mouth.

"You two were almost late."

"But we weren't," Janet told her.

"Almost is the same thing as being late," she said as she stepped aside to let us in. Obviously feeling she had lived long enough in her twenty-five years, Janet dared to respond.

"No, it isn't."

Wow. She went there. I stopped and took a step back, away from Janet, even if it meant staying outside. Captain had gotten out of the truck and cautiously approached, hesitating when he saw my hard reverse. Distraction!

"Gran! I picked up a hostage on my way here. Do you mind feeding him while he waits for rescue?"

Janet, having realized her impending doom, let out a huge breath as Gran's attention was diverted to the detective.

"Lark! Is that the movie star? The one with the flag clothes from that movie you took us to go see?"

Ha! Not the only one.

Gran's face flushed as she studied the prime specimen in front of her. Even frustrated from my stubborn refusal to take him back to his car, he was gorgeous, his hair ruffled from running his hands through it in between texts. Yep. Get him the costume and he could win a look-alike costume against the real actor.

"Gran, may I introduce Detective Brecken Wilson from San Francisco. Detective, this is my grandmother. And my cousin, Janet."

"Her much younger, single cousin," Janet added.

Brat. This would be the last time I helped her. I glared as she pushed past me to shake his hand and turned just in time to see Captain's eyes widen. His body recoiled from the motivated blur of a girl heading towards him.

"Hi. You are from San Francisco?"

Even I winced from her greetings. Poor, overly composed, stoic Brecken stood helpless, trying to find an escape before answering her.

"I am now. My parents followed my sister there a few years ago, and I followed them." He looked over at me, his eyes still wide enough to see white all the way around.

Janet snagged his arm and reeled him closer until his arm was snuggled under her boobs as she leaned closer to hear what I could hear just fine from four feet away.

"Really? How fascinating," she purred. Actually purred. Wow. "Where were you from before that?"

He looked at me again, his eyes begging me to help, but I was still smarting over his insistence on calling me 'Larklyn.' He was on his own.

"Back East." His voice was short and abrupt. He

turned back to Gran, trying to use it as an excuse to put some distance between him and Janet. "Hello, ma'am. Thank you for having me."

"Well aren't you a charmer? You don't see manners like that out here often," she murmured as he shook her hand. If she swooned, I would lose it. "Larklyn, how did you meet such a nice gentleman?"

"He's a detective, Gran. As in investigating the leg. And the arm. In fact, the whole body. Have you found the body yet?" I asked him.

"Larklyn! We don't mention such things in public," Gran chided me as she encouraged Captain into the house. They left Janet behind as Gran took her spot beside him and showed off her house.

"I would argue, but I can see her point. No more body references," I defended myself to Janet, who just looked up at me and rolled her eyes.

Janet and I trailed Gran and Brecken. Gran had an older home, built when the town was founded in the 1950s. It was a cottage style like mine, but whereas mine was small, compact, and comfortable, hers was large, two stories with an attic.

It had a warm, elegant charm, and she loved to use it to entertain, which showed. The easy flow of one room to another, and the large kitchen that could easily fit four cooks, making the house an ideal meeting place for when she held the Sewing Circle gatherings. Which she did, more than her fair share. I couldn't recall how many times I would come to pick up Hailey to find four women, each with her own specialty, arguing over their section of the kitchen. Even though they always ended up in the same spot anyways. Gran would use the oven, making her famous mac & cheese with breadcrumbs. Benny's wife, Alice, would claim the island for the dish of the week, and Sally Mae and Gladys would portion off the leftover counter spaces for their food.

Brecken listened, responding as Gran led him from spot to spot, stopping for too long at the family photos. I closed my eyes, trying to remember what photos were there, but it had been too long since I had noticed, and I never brought people over who would care. Lesson learned. Aunt Helen and Uncle Flynn stood up from where they were waiting in the living room and walked over. Uncle Flynn stopped on his way, snagging two beers for Janet and me.

"Lark, why didn't you tell me you were bringing a boy?" Aunt Helen asked when they got close enough to talk without being overheard by Gran and Brecken.

"I didn't. I kidnapped a detective when he insisted on questioning me tonight instead of tomorrow morning like I told him to."

"Yeah," Janet interrupted. "We need to talk about you withholding the fact that Captain America was investigating you."

"What's there to tell? He's here because the victim was his cousin. For some reason, he thought I was the missing link." Which, now that I thought about it, might have been correct. Also, now that she was using the nickname as well, it seemed... less special. Maybe I should start calling him by his name instead. Nickname officially retired.

"Is he single? I mean, I didn't see a ring, but you

never know these days," Janet asked, drowning out her mother who closed her mouth and rolled her eyes at her daughter.

"Yes, he is single," I answered by habit and then cringed. *Son of a donkey.*

"So, you already asked, huh? I'll back off if you're interested. You aren't getting any younger and your pickings are slim." Janet looked over at him and pursed her lips. "Okay, maybe I will try less aggressively. When they're *that* cute, you have to at least try."

"Thanks," I said with my own eye roll. "I can feel the love."

She clinked our beers together with no effort from me.

"May the best girl win," she said, before downing the rest of her beer and strolling over to Gran and Brecken with a seductive smile.

"Doesn't that behavior bother you?" I asked Aunt Helen, thinking of how I lived in fear of my daughter acting like... well, Janet. I loved my cousin, and she was an amazing interior decorator, but she was also a horrible judge of character, a flake, and someone who made terrible life decisions. All of which were how she got stuck back at home at twenty-five, redoing the summer homes of Barrow Bay's rich instead of in San Francisco where she had started.

Then again, so was I, only I had a divorce under my belt and a child. Glass houses and stones came to mind.

"Yes, but she's an adult. IF SHE WANTS TO ACT LIKE A WHORE, she can." Aunt Helen raised her voice so that Janet could hear her across the room. It worked, as she forgot Brecken when she turned to address her mother.

"I DO NOT ACT LIKE A WHORE!" she screamed back, not bothering to cross the room and argue like a reasonable human being.

"You sure? Because flirting with your cousin's date certainly qualifies," my Aunt fired back. Brecken and I turned bright red in unison at this, and I stumbled to interrupt.

"He's not... we're not... she's fine," I told my Aunt, hoping while already knowing it was too late. I shot a look at Brecken to ask forgiveness before we got too far out of control.

"Did you come together in the same car?" my aunt demanded.

"Yes, but only because—"

"Then it's a date. I don't understand why you young people have to make this so difficult. Just admit you like each other and move on. Don't spend weeks pussy-footing around it."

"Because we don't like—"

"Please! He's gorgeous. Like movie star quality. What's there not to like?"

I saw Brecken go another shade darker in a blush and shift his weight.

"Well, there's the whole 'he thinks I might be involved in a crime' thing—"

"Oh please." My aunt waved this excuse off like an annoying mosquito in summer. "If he thought you were a criminal, he wouldn't be going to a family event with you. Plus, he already knows about the divorce and the child, and he's still around. Don't blow it by pretending to be hard to get."

"No, no… He thought… he didn't come with me, I kidnapped him… like, really kidnapped him. I…" How did this happen? "I'm not playing hard to get!" Well, that sounded better in my mind.

"Damn. Giving it out already? I thought this was your first date," Janet said, her shoulders drooping before abandoning Brecken in favor of another beer.

"We… I… It's not… Oh my god." I gave up and sank into the couch Aunt Helen had just abandoned, burying my head in my hands. "I'm sorry, Brecken. You were right. I should have driven you to your car instead of being on time to dinner," I mumbled into my hands.

"It's… um… yeah…" Brecken stumbled to a stop, looking a little white around his face.

"Look at them. They're so in sync! Already talking the same. It's so cute." My aunt gushed, and then grabbed a plate of cheese and offered one to him. He took it before heading over to sit next to me on the couch. I still had my head in my hands trying to figure out why I thought this would be a good idea.

"So, are we heading out, or should I get ready for your big play?" he asked, lounging on the couch munching on his piece of cheese.

"My big play?" I repeated, pulling my hands down two inches so I could see him.

"Yep. Your big play to get me. Since you aren't playing hard to get," he clarified with a satisfied smirk. He looked completely relaxed. In fact, this was the most relaxed I had seen him since meeting him. It made him sexier.

Sweet cheese and crackers. I returned my head to my hands since teasing me wasn't important enough for eye contact.

"This was not how this was supposed to go," I mumbled.

"How did this go in your head?" His voice was amused.

"*You* were supposed to be embarrassed. *You* were supposed to regret forcing your way into my life. This was supposed to be *you.*" I took one hand down to gesture at myself before giving up and removing the other. There was no point in hiding my face. It couldn't get any more embarrassing. Sitting back, comfortably reclined, he followed my hand down my body and his eyes got stuck on my legs. I hoped. Because that was when I realized I was still in my breeches. Skin-tight beige breeches that hid nothing.

Never mind. It could get worse.

I turned another shade redder and jumped up. "Gran! I didn't have time to change when I left the barn. Can I change into some clean clothes?" At least ones that didn't show off my cellulite. Every molecule in my body was aware of the fact I had to walk away from him, with my breeches showing my assets off to Brecken, who was at eye height to my butt. I didn't look to see if he was watching my exit. I didn't know what I wanted more: him to be looking, or him to not be looking.

"Sure, sweetie, sure. We'll keep your man

company."

My man? Sweet cheese and crackers.

I risked a look back at Brecken, but he smiled at me, no sign of embarrassment on his face. *Snickerdoodles.* I really hadn't thought this through. I took the stairs two at a time and went into the guest room I normally used. Since coming here straight from the barn was not unusual, I kept a change of clothing here for emergencies. Five minutes later, I emerged in clean jeans, a t-shirt with a Hogwarts logo I refused to be embarrassed about, and another pair of tennis shoes. Grabbing my dirty clothing, I walked out to my truck to throw them in the back seat, when Gran startled me.

"Do we need to call the lawyers?" Her face pinched and her hands clasped in front of her. Her grip was so tight with worry that her knuckles were turning white.

"I don't think so. Blake didn't ask many questions, so I was vague. I already called my divorce lawyer and told her everything. She asked me to keep her in the loop, but she wasn't too worried. Blake isn't interested in playing full-time Dad. He was always more of the fun-time guy."

"We need to make this go away. You need to stop those deliveries." She frowned and all the wrinkles from a lifetime of laughter stood out in the dark.

"Brecken and John are working on it. They got a big break in the case today, so soon."

Gran nodded while she took in a deep breath and let it out. "Okay. If you are stopping the deliveries, we will be okay."

I reached out to take her hand in mine, biting back

my denial of any control over the maniac body dumper who was terrorizing my home. Years of dealing with Gran had taught me denial never worked after she had assigned responsibility. In her world I just needed to fix it. Problem solved. I wished the real world and hers coincided more.

"Whoever's doing this will get caught soon. Dropping off body parts is just challenging the police to find you." I smiled as broadly as I could, hoping the size of my smile would translate to confidence. It looked like it worked, because she returned it before switching our roles and grabbing my arm.

"So, tell me about your man."

Well, I knew why she grabbed my arm. It was so I couldn't run.

"He isn't my man. He's here for the case and then he's leaving."

"Men don't just come to family events like this if they aren't interested."

"Yes, they do. Especially when I refused to let him go back to get his car. If Judy hadn't needed supplies for tomorrow, John would have already picked him up."

"Oh, please. Judy bought all her supplies for tomorrow two days ago. She's at home cooking right now while John watches the game."

What?

That little liar.

I grabbed my phone and texted him.

Me: *John! I thought you told Brecken you couldn't pick him up.*

John: *Nope, sorry. Took Judy to the store for tomorrow.*

Me: *Oh please. Gran outed you. You're both at home.*

As I waited for the reply, I heard Gran's phone beep. She looked down at it and smiled, then texted back. I stared at the interaction in shock. Did they... and she smiled... then just responded... *Goodness gracious great balls of fire.* I was ready for this week to end. My phone beeped.

John: *We need a new Chief. He needs a reason to stay. Go get him, tiger.*

My jaw dropped along with my phone after reading that.

Did they... I... no... but...

My mind came up with one answer: run. I turned to make a dash for the truck, but Gran was ahead of me. Grabbing the back of my pants, she dragged me into the house backwards, me wheeling my arms trying to keep balance. It worked until we got to the doorway where I could grab the frame and hold on, her yanking and me pulling towards freedom.

"Larklyn Davis! How old are you?"

"Coming from the person dragging me in, that question loses it punch!"

"Larklyn! You are thirty years old and the mother of a seven-year-old. Act like it!"

"No. I will not do it! I am not some police whore you can sell for a good position and two cows!"

"Please! I love you, Larklyn, but you have more debt than income. Who would offer two cows for you?" Gran replied, yanking again. This time my right hand came loose, sending both of us back a few inches before my left could adjust. I swung my right out, trying to catch the ledge again, but the lost inches were making it impossible.

"Who's buying Larklyn?" The voice belonged to the last person I wanted to hear our conversation. Brecken's amused question got us both to stand up. I grabbed my pants and pulled them up from where they had slipped down in the altercation and tried to act normal.

"Nothing." Said in stereo, the 'nothing' sounded suspicious, even to my ears, and he lifted an eyebrow up while watching us.

"Really?" He put a lot of weight into the word and we both blushed.

Well, Gran blushed. I started to, then got distracted by the sight of my seventy-eight-year-old grandmother, who discussed *Sixty Shades of Grey* in her sewing group last month, blush like a virgin. Wait... I meant fifty. Or was it forty? Yep, I was over here keeping up with the times.

"Nothing. No one is selling anyone. Larklyn was just being overdramatic," Gran said, waving her hand and walking back into the house. Seeing a possible escape route and not having much self-respect left after this week, I turned back towards the truck only to have her snag my arm and pull me after her again.

Sigh.

"Brecken, just out of curiosity, can they charge me with a crime if I run away and the old person won't let go? I mean, I didn't hurt them. It was their own actions that caused the injuries. I wouldn't get in trouble, right?"

"Lark, I don't think the police will be your issue. Once she recovers, she'll come after you herself, and she seems to be a very relentless woman." He couldn't hide his laughter as he answered. At least someone was having a good time.

"Good point." I gave in to the situation and followed meekly. My grandmother led us to the dining room to a table covered in food.

"Gran! This is like a four-course meal! Why did you make all this food?"

"Larklyn! We have guests," she hissed.

"Yeah, but you didn't know he was coming when you…" That sneaky witch. How did she know I would kidnap him? "You know what? Never mind. I'm just going to sit down and not talk to anyone."

"Oh please, Lark. You wouldn't want your beau to think you're rude," Aunt Helen said.

I leveled her a look, trying to make it clear I knew what they were doing. And I wasn't buying. Aunt Helen was unrepentant. She just kept dishing up items, giving Brecken the prime portions with a happy smile that he returned. In fact, he seemed remarkably laid-back and amused, his shoulders relaxed. I included him in my glare, but when he noticed, all I got was a bigger grin. *Donkey's butt.*

"So, you're from back east?" my Aunt asked, encouraging Brecken to talk about himself.

He looked over at me for a second before answering and I blushed.

"Yeah, my family grew up in the Boston area. I did my graduate studies at Harvard before I went into the

NYPD."

"You were in the NYPD?" I asked, my head sinking to the side as I tried to understand.

"Yeah, but it wasn't for me. I was only in for about four years before my sister... well, when she got divorced the whole family wanted to be closer to her. So, I quit. Then my old boss found me a job with the Sheriff's department in San Francisco, and that's where I've been since."

"Wow. That's an impressive story, Brecken. And it's so amazing that your family wanted to stay so close to your sister. The TV makes it seem like few families are that close these days," Aunt Helen commented.

"Yeah. She has a son and needed the help. We also wanted to know him better, and we were struggling from where we were."

"Can I ask why she didn't move to you?" I asked.

"She... It wasn't possible." His answer was short, and I got the impression that there was more there, but he didn't want to talk about it. "What about you, Lark? What brought you to Barrow Bay from San Fran?"

"My parents died. Car accident." I didn't mean to have such a short answer, but my throat clamped up and I sat taking deep gasping breaths, trying to get past it.

"I'm sorry. I shouldn't have asked."

"No. It's fine. I just miss them. We were close even though they hated Blake. They weren't surprised at all when I found out he was cheating." Wow. Five sentences and I brought up my dead parents, my ex, and how he cheated on me. Maybe Jen was right about needing to work on my flirting. I looked around at my family, hoping someone might have something to distract him with, but they all were watching the two of us like we were a TV show. Fabulous.

"He was cheating?" Brecken's voice pulled my attention back to him. And his pity. Deep breath.

"With his assistant trainer. That's the horse world's version of sleeping with his secretary." I didn't bother hiding my disgust. He could have at least been sleeping with one of his hotter students. His assistant trainer wasn't even attractive. It was a double hit to my ego.

"He's an idiot," Brecken said with a smile. Butterflies in my stomach went wild, and I took my gaze down to my plate in an attempt to calm them down.

"Yep," I replied.

"So, tell me about how you found your place out here," he asked. Everyone was still watching our interaction without interrupting.

"Manipulation." I sent Gran a teasing glare. "Gran invited Hailey and me back for a few weeks after my parents passed to get us away from the memories. Next thing I know, the Chief was showing me how to get my business license for the town, Judy was showing me properties, and Gran had a contractor out to show me the plans for my new barn. I resisted until I found my house, though. Gran drove me by it, and it was magic. It spoke to me."

"We knew what you and Hailey needed. We found it for you. That's what a good family does," Gran said with a firm nod and a soft smile.

"I'm pretty sure you mean bossy family, but it's worked out, so I won't complain."

"Maybe you should remember that. Family knows best," Gran threw in.

"I think you got lucky," I shot back.

"Things happen for a reason."

"Oh no. No! This did not happen for a reason. I refuse. No way." I slammed my hands down on the table. Fate did not send body parts to start up romance. Nope.

"I think she doth protest too much," Janet threw in with an evil smile.

I hated that line. There was no good response. Protest, you lose. Agree, you lose.

"Detective? You done with your meal? I can take you home now," I told him, pulling my napkin from my lap and putting it down on the table.

"He's back to 'Detective.' She's trying to avoid this," Janet commented.

"I'm actually not done—" Brecken protested while I glared.

"Good. Let's go." I got up before Brecken could get his mouth closed.

"No, really, I'm not—"

"Time to go!"

He finally took me seriously and shoveled food in as he slowly got up, grabbing two biscuits as he followed me out.

"Your grandmother is a good cook," he commented as we got in the truck.

"Yep."

"Your answers always get short when you're uncomfortable or mad."

I swallowed hard and kept my eyes from looking at him. Stupid detectives with their stupid observational skills.

"Yep."

"So, when we first met, where you uncomfortable or mad?"

"Yep."

He thought about that for a second, and I could feel his gaze studying my profile even though I refused to look.

"Okay then."

"Okay then," I echoed. Except I did not understand what was okay.

I was in so much trouble.

CHAPTER 10

The ride back to Brecken's car was quiet as we both contemplated today's discoveries. Granted, his were probably more important, with the whole murder and drugs and all that, but my family actively setting me up was just as big in my world. I mean, I wasn't that girl anymore. I didn't know how to 'hook up' or... oh my god, kiss. Do kissing techniques change over time? No, no, that was just silly.

Wasn't it?

It wasn't until he was about to get out that I summoned the courage to speak.

"Sorry about tonight. I should have just insisted we talked tomorrow. Or after the dinner."

"Then I wouldn't know about Annie Phan. That was worth the dinner." For some reason that made my stomach drop. He had a bad time at dinner. Something made my chest cramp and I tried to figure out why his agreement with my own assessment hurt.

Oh no. I remembered this feeling.

This was disappointment. Hurt. Hope crushed under the soles of polite words. All emotions I should not be feeling.

Mayday. Mayday.

"Well, I'm glad it worked out for you," I answered, falling back on manners when panic removed any chance at snark.

"I'm sorry that the dinner didn't work out for you. And that you didn't get your pho."

"I'm never going to get pho in town again, am I?" I couldn't help the pathetic whimper that escaped.

"Who knows? Maybe a nice Vietnamese family might move in. One that doesn't sell drugs."

"So, no. Fiddlesticks. I would have savored that last bowl longer had I known."

"Maybe I'll have to get you one to make up for it. The next time you're in the city, that is." He turned red and shot me a quick look before dropping his gaze to the truck door. "Well, anyway, thanks for... everything. Bye."

I watched him get out and get in his car without moving, my mouth hanging slightly open as I tried to get past my own insecurities to grasp what he said. His taillights were long gone before I could process it.

Did I just get asked out?

Maybe?

I wasn't sure. It had been a long time.

No, maybe he was just making up for the loss of my pho connection.

I swallowed hard and went to put my truck in reverse when there was a shadow. For once, I had the correct reaction.

I screamed.

My hand scrambled to grab the gear shift, slamming

my knuckles into the dashboard instead, before catching my target on the bounce.

"Ouch! Donkey droppings!"

The shadow moved closer to my truck. I closed my hand around the gear stick and pulled desperately, searching for the right gear to get me out of here.

There. No! That was park! Try again. There. The gear locked in and...

I was in neutral.

NO!

My eyes bulged as I realized I was going to die. And that I owed Hollywood a few apologies. At least in slasher movies the worthless female lead struggled with the lock. Or even turning the car on. Me? I had already achieved those hurdles, only to die because I couldn't panic and shift at the same time. I was truly pathetic. My ex-mother-in-law was right. I wasn't qualified to raise a child. Or be an adult. Or—

"Lark? Honey? Are you okay?" I turned and let out another scream when I saw a face in the window. Annie's face. Her face was scrunched up in concern and she knocked again as I tried to calm myself. If she was less than a foot away, she probably wouldn't kill me. Probably. I mean, it would be a struggle to even bring a gun up to fire at this range.

What was I supposed to do? Should I roll down the window and play dumb? Or was this just a way to lure me into a false sense of security before she knocked me off?

Oh, Lord. I've been watching too much TV. I rolled down the window, plastering a smile on my face and hoped she missed the panic in my eyes.

"Sorry, Annie. I... It was dark, and you startled..."
I was breathless as my chest hadn't gotten the all-clear
message yet.

"No worry. I was just leaving you a note when I saw
you drive up." She held up a folded paper and my blood
pressure jumped. She had to have seen Brecken.

"Yeah, I guess you saw Detective Wilson. He came
with me to Gran's house."

"Oh, I know." Her grin was evil. Pure amused evil.
Oh no.

She held up her phone and turned it so I could see.
Has Lark found a man? The words flashed at the top
of her phone. Oh god. Didn't Lindsey have a life? And
how did she find out about these things so quickly? My
fear forgotten, my head slumped towards the steering
wheel as I contemplated how much effort it would take
to move to another town. Maybe one not so small.
Somewhere far away.

"I wouldn't have panicked if I had known he was
your beau," she added, smirking at my discomfort.

"Yes, you would have." I thought. Oh god. I said
that. Out loud. I was going to die tonight. Where was
my cell phone? For the love of—I had a cell phone. Why
didn't it occur to me to try calling someone earlier?
Hopefully Hailey got her dad's survival skills because
mine were failures.

Annie just grinned.

"Recognized me, did he? It's been a while since
anyone's cared about little old me." Her innocent tone
made me look up from my place of shame.

"I care! I care about my pho. And our teas in the garden. I love that garden!" I protested before slapping my hand over my mouth. "Oh my god. That sounded so selfish. And crazy. Full out crazy. I meant that I cared about our friendship." It came out a little muffled through my fingers, but she smiled anyway.

"You are such a sweet girl, Lark."

I snorted.

"Dang. It's been years since anyone has called me a girl."

"Haha! In my family you are a girl until your mother dies, and by then you've become an old lady."

I laughed hard. Too hard for the joke, tears coming to my eyes. All my stress and nerves came out, taking over my body. Annie watched, her eyebrows meeting her hair line before she smiled as well.

"You are not okay. You know this, right?" she asked me through her grin.

I nodded through the laughter as I tried to pull in enough air to stop.

"That ... has ... been made ... clear ... this week."

She nodded, holding her laughter in. Like an adult. Go her.

"So, do you want to talk about today?"

"When you yelled 'cop' at me and slammed the door?"

"Pretty much."

"Yeah, that was disappointing. I really wanted some pho."

"You were going to your grandmother's for dinner."

"I love pho," I whined.

"You have a problem. You should look into it."

"That depends on if you're leaving or not. Do I have a problem?" Please don't leave. I needed my hook up. Also, I was completely selfish. At this point I was just embracing it.

"No, no. I stay. This is my home." Annie shook her head with her denial.

"But, what about—?"

"I'm retired. I come here to make a new life. I have nothing to run from."

"So, you are not a drug dealer?" My system was calming down, and I put my hand on my chest to help. "Thank the lords."

"Not anymore."

Well, shiitake mushrooms.

"I didn't hear that," I countered. "Let's leave me with plausible deniability, okay?" She smiled as she nodded.

"*If* I was a drug dealer in this area, and I heard about another, more… infamous drug dealer moving into the area, I might want to… ensure my hold on the area." She was thinking through her phrasing, pursing her lips while looking for the right word. "And *if* there was a… problem… in my current supply chain, I might—what is the phrase I am thinking about? There is killing, and two things…"

"Kill two birds with one stone?"

"Yes."

"Okay then." My mind was reeling with the possibilities. What would Brecken want to know next, other than the name of the killer? Or Bryan's supplier. "Supposing that this infamous drug dealer was in the area, would they still be in the game enough to know the players?"

"Only the local contact. Bryan was… obvious. And a slut. Wait, we call them man-whores now, right? Either way, he was a flirt, and leading people on has a way of catching up with you." Annie nodded a goodbye before handing me the note and walking away. I watched until she disappeared into the dark, only to see headlights seconds later. She must have parked near the room that may one day be my office. I watched until the car passed me and turned onto the road.

It was official. I was friends with a drug dealer. A retired big-time drug dealer.

I looked at the paper in my hand and frowned. Did I want to know? I didn't, but I also couldn't handle not knowing. I mentally cursed myself as I unfolded the paper.

Fiona Miller

I had no idea. None. I stared for a few more minutes before putting my truck in reverse and pulling out. Which I could do. Now. Since no one was trying to kill me. Sigh.

***

I made it home without another incident and, as I pulled into the garage, I sat for a second, praying that tomorrow would be normal. I couldn't do it. Not another day like today. Annie's visit had made that clear. My survival instincts were horrible.

My phone rang, and I stared at it, trying to get in the mental space to talk with Hailey.

"Hello, Sweetpea. How are you doing? Are you having fun with your dad?"

"Yep! We went riding and everything today. Daddy told me that I was going to stay here this weekend instead of coming home."

"Yeah, I thought you might want to spend more time there before school starts up. Is that okay?"

"Well, Daddy said he would take me to the festival this weekend, so I guess it's alright."

"Good, good. I'm glad you're going to have some fun together." I sounded tired to my own ear, and I tried to brighten my voice for the next part. "Have you seen your grandmother?"

"What's wrong, Mommy?" My daughter's voice was firm. Maybe I shouldn't have tried for the fake happy. It was overkill.

"Nothing, Sweetpea. Just missing you."

"Maybe I should come home Saturday."

"NO!" Keep it cool. Keep it cool. "No, no. I'm fine. You and your dad need more time together."

"Okay, if you are really okay—" Dang. My daughter was insightful. I was unsure if I was more proud or irritated.

"I'm fine, Hailey Bailey. Don't worry about me. I'll see you the weekend after next."

"Bye, Mommy!"

"Bye, Sweetpea." I pressed the disconnect button in time to catch the tear on my face. With all the excitement of the past few days, I had been able to distract myself from how much I missed my daughter. Now all the emotions rushed in and made me almost double over with longing. I needed my little girl back. This case needed to be wrapped up so she could come home.

But how?

I thought about all the information I knew.

Bryan Wilson was a barista and drug dealer that worked at Tops.

Based on his car and home, he had been a successful one.

He was dating two women at once that we knew about, maybe more.

He was a local with a questionable history but had been flying under the radar here for years. Or had he? Maybe it was time to hit up the Sewing Group.

God save my soul. And ears.

I pulled out my phone and texted Gran.

Me: *Hey Grandma. Just wondering if you wanted company tomorrow…*

Gran: *You aren't avoiding a date, right?*

For the love of—

Me: *No. There is no date. There will be no date. Not until Hailey is older.*

This must have upset her because it took forever for her to text me back.

Gran: *Ok. Meet me at my house at five.*

I mentally ran through my schedule for tomorrow. I could do that. I might not get lunch, but I could do that.

Me: *See you then.*

Gran: *Oh, and please shower this time. Can't have the girls thinking I didn't raise my family right and you stank tonight.*

Oh my god. She told me this now. What did Brecken think? Wait! No. I didn't care what he thought. I was not that girl. I was not interested in dating. I was an independent, successful woman.

I sniffed.

Whew. Who stank.

I really needed to revisit my idea of successful.

CHAPTER 11

The next morning, I woke up in my own bed for the first time in days. I let myself lay there, cozy in my comfort, trying to ignore my responsibilities. Finally pulling myself from my blankets, I walked to my coffee maker in my tank top and pajamas shorts, reveling in the freedom to wear what I wanted. The bottoms were really plaid-printed booty shorts pretending to be pajamas, that I rationalized wearing because I was in my own house. No one was around to see my cellulite or butt cheeks. My modesty was secure.

Knock. Knock.

Oh no. No, no, no.

I went to my front door and peered out the peephole. No one. Wait. Was that John's car? And Brecken's? Maybe. They were common cars. I didn't see anyone, though. Okay, I was only on my first cup but I knew I heard some—

Knock, knock.

I spun, trying to find the noise. After a few frazzled turns, I had narrowed it down to the back door. I approached carefully, dragging my feet, which seemed to have found the self-preservation instinct that was missing last night.

"Hello?" I tried to call out with confidence, but the shaking in my voice told them everything they needed to know.

"Hey, Lark! It's John and Brecken. We... need to talk."

Nope.

"I'm sorry. You have reached Lark's... automated home... butler. She is away from the house right now. Please leave a message or come back later." Hey, it was worth a try.

"Lark, open up. Preferably before you try to walk out the front door."

Well, I had to give it to them. That got my door open so fast I hit my foot when I didn't move it fast enough.

"Ouch — What do you mean I shouldn't go out my front door?" I demanded, shaking my injured foot out while I stared at them. John's eyebrows crept up for a second before his eyes dropped down and then back up as he started... coughing? Or laughing. Or hiding his laughter in a coughing fit, which is where I put my bet. I narrowed my eyes at him before I turned my glare to Brecken. Who was still looking down. At my legs? Why would...

Oh no.

My instinct was to mimic his look, but the part of me that was awake forced my eyes closed. If I didn't look maybe I could pretend I didn't just answer my door in booty shorts and a tank top. With no bra.

I had to look.

Screaming, I slammed the door in their faces, one hand clasped against my mouth to stop any other embarrassing sounds and the other across my chest. Fear had the same response as cold. And arousal. Enough said.

Find a leg on my porch? No scream. Answer the door in practically nothing to find the hottest man I have ever seen in real life? Scream. Maybe my mother dropped me on my head as a child.

"What do you mean I shouldn't go out my front door?" I yelled again through the door, trying to recover from my embarrassment.

"Um… do you think you might put some clothes on? We need to talk." I was about to open my mouth in agreement when Brecken continued. "And don't open your front door."

"You guys realize that now that you've said three times *not* to open my door, I want to open my front door?" Reverse psychology was surprisingly tempting. Now that they had made a big deal about it, I wanted to know what it was.

"I would trust us on this. Don't."

"Fine. Give me a minute."

"Take your time," Brecken responded.

I paused. "Really? Can I take a shower while you wait out there?" I couldn't believe that came out of my mouth. Something about Brecken just brought out the imp in me.

"We would prefer if you didn't," his response drifted through the door. "It's a little chilly this morning."

"Okay. Be right back."

A few minutes later I had armored myself in the biggest sweatshirt I had, and a pair of loose jeans I kept around for my fat days. I was one chastity belt away from declaring I would never have sex again. Feeling less revealed, I headed back to the back door and opened it.

"Hey," I greeted.

Both detectives nodded, John with a grin that told me he probably already had texted his wife. *Shiitake balls.* Brecken was fixated on the door jamb, dedicated to avoiding my gaze. Or at least, I assumed so since I was doing a pretty good job of avoiding his gaze, too.

"Can we come in?" John asked.

"Sure. Coffee?"

"Some of your gourmet coffee?" John asked, his eyes swinging to mine as his smile widened. "I would love some."

Sigh. Being nice to cops was getting expensive.

"Brecken?"

"Sure," he grunted, his eyes still looking anywhere but at me.

"You also a masochist like John?"

"Only when desperate. I would love some cream if you have it."

"Sweet cream work?"

"Perfect."

I led them into the kitchen and indicated they should sit down while I made three more cups of coffee. This seemed like a two-cup discussion. By the time all the coffee was made and I was sitting at the table, both of my morning cups in front of me, I heard a commotion outside. My head snapped to look at the front of the yard but John stopped me from getting up with a hand on my arm.

"Lark, we need to tell you…" He stopped and just patted my arm for a few seconds.

"For monkey's ears, John. Just get it out. The situations that are going through my head are giving me a panic attack." Really, I was having flashbacks to my parents' deaths. I didn't know what they had come to tell me, but the phrasing was too similar to the horrible memories.

"You had another delivery. This morning Bryan's body was delivered to your front yard, behind some of your bushes."

No one was dead. No one new, at least. Okay. I could handle… wait.

NO.

"Umm. No."

"We—I'm sorry, did you just say, 'no'?" John asked, his head tilting in surprise.

"Yep. No. No more deliveries. They were supposed to go to another house. Who could be so stupid to not know that they have the WRONG ADDRESS? Now they are messing with my job. My reputation! No. No more. End it. Today."

I couldn't stop myself from standing at the end of my rant. To calm myself, I walked to the sink, only to realize I didn't have anything in it to clean. The one time I need dirty dishes and I had to be responsible the night before. Taking a deep breath, I turned to face them just in time to catch them sharing a look. One I had seen too many times this week.

"Just spill it. I don't know how much more I can take."

"There was a note."

Okay. That wasn't what I was expecting.

"A note." That reminded me. I still needed to tell them about Annie's note.

"Yes. Addressed to you."

Annie's note was forgotten. "To me." *Son of a donkey's uncle.*

"Yes." John sat there waiting for me to speak. I stood there waiting for him to have a punchline. Because that had to be a joke. Our standoff went on for a minute before I gave in.

"I got a note. From the killer. On Bryan's body." Even summarized, it didn't sound good.

"Well, the note is on your front door with a picture of the body and the body is behind your bushes in the front yard, but either way, yes."

"Okay." They both stared at me, waiting. "What? Until you tell me what's in the note, I have nothing to add." Don't ask... don't ask... "Is the picture of the body before the amputations or after? No! Don't answer that. I don't want to know. Okay, I do. No!" Oh goodness gracious. I had gone off my rocker. Completely crazy. I needed to sit down. And slam my head against the table a few times.

"Lark. Are you okay?" Brecken asked, walking towards me with his arms out like he was going to comfort me.

"No!" I glared at them from where I sat in my chair.

"Some idiot is leaving me bodies! On purpose! Like, here. You look like *you* need an arm. The killer is like the Oprah of body parts. You get an arm. And you get an arm." Brecken opened his mouth to speak, and I put my hand up. "I know, I know. I have been the only person to receive body parts. But multiple deliveries should count." Deep breaths. "Okay. What did it say?"

"Stop involving the cops."

My brain stopped. Like a car stalling before the engine caught again.

"Are they stupid? Is this a joke? No. They have to be stupid. How would I not involve the police? What? Do they think I'm secretly a ninja? Horse trainer by day, super sleuth at night? *Of course* I'm going to call the cops! That's a threat! I'm going to go to the cops for protection. I don't even know how to punch someone! There's something about how to make a fist and if you do it wrong, then you can break your thumb, but I don't know what it is!" At some point I had jumped to my feet again, knocking the chair back as I waved my hands to emphasize my rant.

"Okay, do you want the rest of the note or do you want to yell some more?" John asked.

There's more?

"Why did you hesitate if there was more?" I asked. Okay. I might have yelled a little, but I tried to ask. It was the thought that counted.

"You didn't let me. I paused for dramatic effect and then you were off." John shook his head at me. I was too anxious to sit, so I just stood, my arms crossed, waiting.

"Fine. Go."

"The note continued, saying, 'If you don't get out of the area, you will join your dealer.'"

"*My* dealer."

"Yep."

"They still think *I'm* Annie?" My voice broke which reminded me to calm down and breathe. Okay. Adult. I was an adult. I trained 1,200-pound animals that find ways to injure themselves in strange and inventive ways frequently. I could handle this. Deal with the threat first.

"Okay, so isn't this where the young, handsome detective promises to protect me with his life? That he won't leave my side until I'm safe?" Oh wait. That wasn't supposed to come out of my mouth. But judging from the faces in front of me, it did. In my mind, I was slapping the back of my head for stupidity. And maybe being a tad bit more honest than I wanted to be.

"Pretty sure that's you, Brecken," John volunteered with a chuckle. Brecken and I both glared.

"No! Sorry. My brain goes to sarcasm when stressed. Just ignore that last part."

"I don't know. I think it's a good idea. Brecken, you should stick to Lark like glue." John laughed at our matching horror.

"NO!" Calm. Staying calm. "I mean, no, Brecken's too talented to waste following me around. It was a joke. A joke!" *Fudge buckets.* If he was close to me, I would be tempted to do something stupid. Like kiss him.

Or more. More sounded good. Too good.

Leaving. He was leaving. And eventually the body

parts had to stop. They were out of them at this point.

Wait.

They. *They* would run out.

"Could it be multiple people?"

The detectives looked up at me.

"What do you mean?" Brecken asked. I looked at him, which was a mistake. My previous thoughts flooded my brain, and I averted my eyes, hiding my blush and trying to get the attention off me as quickly as possible.

"Never mind. It was stupid. They are probably just from out of town." They both stared at me with their eyes wide. "Umm, did I say something?"

"Out of town."

"She's right. They have to be from out—"

"Then maybe—" They seemed to be having their own conversation, obviously following some extension of my thought, but I wasn't privy to it.

"Okay. I'm going to let you talk. Mind if I take a shower?" All I got was an absent hand wave as I left the room. Well. Nice to know they cared about what I was doing. Wait. No. It's good they don't care. Not caring is good. I was just going to ignore the sinking feeling that Brecken didn't care to watch me leave. Attraction. Illogical and powerful. Not what I needed.

This time I packed a suitcase. Once is happenstance. Twice is a coincidence. Three times is enemy action. I was sure my English teacher would be proud of me for thinking of an Ian Fleming quote that quickly. The barn had a living quarters that I used to shower in. I could just stay there. Except that there was no heat. I weighed the benefits and costs between no heat and having to face

Jen's painting for another night.

Wait, they just delivered the body to me. I couldn't bring this to my barn. To where I worked to pay the bills. Nope. Going to the barn until this was solved was out. I'll have Missy cover my rides today and take tomorrow as it came. *Shiitake Mushrooms*. That painting couldn't be that bad. And I could bring coffee. I'd text Jen later. Or—

No.

Anything but that.

Darn. Staying with Gran for the night made the most sense. Okay, okay. I could do it. I was a mother, self-employed and strong. I could survive my grandmother for one night. But only one.

I stalked out of the bedroom dragging my bag behind me as I took out my anger on the two unaware detectives.

"So, does anyone want to tell me why no one was watching my house last night?" Both detectives looked at me, their mouths open. I doubled down on my comment by crossing my arms and lifting my forehead. "I have to say, this is nothing like the movies. You were supposed to be so worried about my safety, or at least catching the criminal, that you should have been outside all night watching. So? Why was no one out there?"

"Because we figured that no one was stupid enough to deliver body parts to the wrong address three times."

"Well! You were wrong!"

"I would like to point out that the body was delivered to your front yard this time. So, technically, we weren't completely wrong," Brecken said.

Wrong move.

"I'm sorry. I thought you said there was a NOTE ON MY DOOR." I was yelling again. This was a blatant example of loss of control. Not good.

"Okay, so that might have been a mistake," Brecken admitted with a one-sided shoulder shrug.

"What's your next brilliant move?"

"Not telling non-police people what we're doing," Brecken answered.

"Yeah, I am going to need more than that. I now have a credible threat against me from a murderer. What are you going to do about it?"

"I'm planning to go with the Hallmark movie option." John, who had been leaning back in his seat, smiling as his gaze hopped between the two of us, threw out that comment. Probably just to escalate the situation for his own amusement. I hope.

"No—"

"Yes. Lark, you are right. You have a—how did you put it? Oh, yeah. Credible threat. You need police protection. For some reason you seem to be in the sights of the killer. Two birds. One stone."

Son of a biscuit.

I *still* hadn't told them about Annie's note. They kept distracting me.

"Um, about two birds—"

"No, Lark. Brecken is going to shadow you all day. The barn should close for the day. You two should go on a date. Be seen around town. See if anyone pays too much attention to you."

Blink, blink.

Oh, my god. John managed to get me a date by body dump. I don't know if I should be impressed or horrified.

John sat, relaxing in the chair as he waited, probably for our protests. Which were coming. I knew I had something. Any second now I was going to have a great excuse why I couldn't go on a fake date with Captain America. Any. Second.

"That doesn't sound… effective?"

John blinked at my attempt as I stumbled to a stop.

"So, I'm going to ignore whatever that was, and say have a great day. Lark, why don't you leave your truck here? That way we will know how close an eye they're keeping on the house. Brecken can drive you around."

Brecken looked like he had swallowed something sour, but he just sat there, not saying a word. I guess he was in.

"Don't bother. We can walk."

"Where are you guys going?" John asked as he interlaced his fingers and grinned.

"We're going to Nuts." I turned to grab my purse and bag. "Should we put this in the back of your car?" I asked Brecken.

"Can we circle around again? How are we going nuts?" Brecken looked lost. Completely lost.

"Well, I'm being driven crazy by a murdering body defiler. I don't know what your excuse is." My snark had returned. Thank goodness.

"She means you two are going to the Nut Shop," John answered for me. Killjoy.

"Why?"

"Because this deserves donuts! Come on." I gestured to get him out the door, but he still stood trying to grasp the puns of small town life.

"No, we really need to go back to why the Nut store had donu—oh. I get it now."

"If it makes you feel better, they also sell nuts."

"At what point did a business decide to sell donuts *and* nuts for a living?"

"One, it's pastries, not just donuts. And two, the name of the place is Dough & Nuts. Clear, concise, and you know what they sell. Good advertising, I think."

"You all are crazy."

"You have no idea," I replied.

CHAPTER 12

Leaving Brecken to contemplate the decisions that led him to this wonderfully crazy town, I grabbed what I assumed were his keys and dragged my bag behind me as I headed to the front door. I was concentrating on texting Missy to not come in today and reading the text from my stall cleaner, Billy, that he had saw a body on my porch this morning when he went to feed. That would teach me to not check my phone first thing. I was concentrating so hard on my phone I almost missed it.

Noises were coming from the other side of the door. *Oh sassafras.*

"Can I go out the front yet?" I stood at the door, glaring for all I was worth at this new annoyance.

"Nope. We are still processing the note. Take the back door." With a long exhale, I turned on my heels and walked through the kitchen to the back door, the men watching. John's smirk seemed to be permanent and inappropriate for the situation, so I gave him my best glare. Since his only reaction was a chuckle, I needed to find a new glare. Mental note — try different glares later in the mirror. There had to be one that worked on unruly policemen.

Brecken watched the interaction with his same confused expression, mouth open like he was going to say something, then closed when John shook his head. I was clearly missing something, but I had passed my level of caring. Let them be cryptic and keep secrets. I was done. My morning was ruined, my coffee was cold, and I just wanted to leave. I ignored them and stormed past, the keys in my hand jiggling with each step. I made it as far as the steps when John called out after me.

"Lark?" Stopping was the only concession I was willing to give to show him I was listening. "Those are my keys. That's why they have a picture of my wife on one of the key chains. Not to mention the BBPD key chain."

Jumping Junipers.

Unwilling to concede my ground, I held them out behind me, keeping my face toward my path. I felt Brecken's heat as he moved behind me and took the keys, their weight leaving my hand as I heard them travel through the air to be caught with another jingle. Brecken's nearness pulled at me and I tried to ignore the lure. The fact I knew it was Brecken told me this 'date' was a horrible idea. I didn't need any help to be even more into this man.

I let him push past me, hyper-focused on how his arm brushed mine and what he meant by it. Did that indicate he might be interested? Or was it just an accident? Or was I obsessing? *Sweet cheese and crackers.* My money was on that last option.

Brecken stopped when he got a few steps in front of

me and I forgot to breathe, my breath stuck in my chest. Was he going to ask me out, like, for real?

"Are you coming or not?" Okay. The romance was dead. I could return to real life.

"I don't know, are you leading?" One brow rose as he assessed my statement. Yeah, yeah. It was stupid. I knew that. Instead of trying again, I walked toward him, gesturing for him to lead. He didn't say anything, which I was grateful for, and in silence we walked to his car where he popped open his trunk and helped me put my stuff in. I followed, trying to subdue the butterflies that popped up in my belly. It had been a while since any man helped me put something, well, anywhere.

We made impressive time to Dough & Nut, and when we walked in, Olivia, one of the co-owners, met us at the register with a huge smile. Olivia was older, maybe in her late fifties, and had been baking since she was younger than me. She had married and had children young, raising them between getting up every day early to run her bakery. Her first husband died of cancer when her kids were still young, and it was tragic, until a few years later James Harrison moved his nuts business into the space next door. One year of fighting turned into twenty years of wedded bliss. On the day they got married, they took out the wall that separated the two shops together. It was one of the most romantic stories I'd heard. The photo of them taking a sledgehammer to the wall hangs behind the register, her in her wedding dress and him in his tux. Sigh. Life goals.

"Lark! How's your house doing? I heard about your troubles." She came out from behind the counter to give me a big hug, one I desperately needed.

"I'm fine. Brecken and John will find them soon. I have faith." Dude. That came out like a heroine in a romance novel... no. I couldn't. I shouldn't. I was going to. I turned to Brecken, grabbing his arm and fluttering my eyelashes up at him. "In fact, Brecken might catch them all by himself, he's such an amazing detective. Have you met Brecken yet? Most handsome man in the Sheriff's department. I just know they'll use him on recruitment posters if they haven't already." His blush told me I struck gold with that guess. Also, I needed to go look up the photos. If there was a calendar with him sans shirt, I was buying it. Supporting our local sheriff's department was important. Very, very important. Was it hot in here? Must be the ovens.

"No." She spoke slowly, giving me a long look before turning to Brecken. "Has anyone mentioned you look just like Captain America?" I had forgotten her husband was a huge Marvel fan. Brecken grew even redder. This was fun.

"No. No one."

Ha! Liar. There was no way people hadn't said it to his face before.

"Brecken here is a hero," I said, with more eye-flutters in his direction after a wink at Olivia.

"No, no I'm not. She would have been fine had I not been there. One of the other guys would have gotten to her." Oh ho! I liked the sound of that story.

"Don't be so humble." I leaned into his arm like I had seen others do (cough, cough, Lindsey) and pressed it to my chest as I doubled down in my smile. His eyes widened, and he looked around for what I assumed was an exit. Not today. Gripping his arm harder to make it clear there was none, I turned to Olivia. "He is so humble. You just can't let him go without him telling you the whole story." He turned to me with panic on his face. I was a horrible person. Horrible, horrible person. "It's a great story."

"It really isn't," he protested. "I was just in the right place at the right time."

"And—" That got me a glare.

"And I was off duty getting some food at Pier 39 when she had just slipped into the water, so I—"

"Oh no! She fell into the bay?" Olivia's eyes widened as she moved closer to hear the rest of the story.

"Well, yes, but—"

"Can you imagine how scary that was?" Olivia asked me. Brecken looked flustered and red. I was having too much fun with this. It was better than the donut.

"She's fine. I checked in with her owner—"

"Her what?!" we both cried in stereo. He grinned. Yeah. He might have won that round after all.

"Her owner. He said that she hurt her paw when she went in, but nothing a few days' rest didn't cure, and she still likes to run off any chance she gets, so no fears."

A dog. He was telling the story about a dog. Goodness gracious. I couldn't help the laugh that slipped out as he continued to tell Olivia the story.

"Then the video went viral and everyone wanted to talk to the cop that saved the pit bull. She was wrapped up around me with her paws around my neck like a person. I should have known it was going to get silly."

Oh my God. I had seen that photo! I just hadn't paid too much attention to the cop. Until now. Brecken Wilson was a man that jumped into the Bay to rescue a drowning pit bull. There went my heart. I had no chance of resisting this man.

Hailey.

Him leaving.

Heart break.

Okay. No, I was right before. No relationships. I was devoted to Hailey first and foremost. I had already learned that broken hearts hurt my ability to take care of my child. I didn't need a second lesson.

"I need coffee." I needed out of here. Between Olivia, with her stupid romantic love story, and Brecken's stupid dog rescue story, I was losing control.

"I thought you wanted a donut?" Brecken asked. I dropped my hold on his arm and moved towards the door.

"Nope. Now I need coffee. Now." I admit I was running, but he was the full package. Gorgeous, brave, smart, and he rescued dogs. Every woman had their weakness. I had just met mine. Now I needed a full retreat. Maybe some aversive shock treatment.

Brecken just followed in my wake as I walked— okay, speed walked—my way to Tops. Since it was the middle of the day, there were only two other people in the store. One walked out as we walked in, so I went straight to the register, leaving Brecken near the door. Laura was talking to the other person, a redhead who was tiny. Impressively tiny. The kind of girl everyday men liked to date so that they could feel like a 'real man' and

show Zach he had won, I walked up the sidewalk to Gran's door. It opened before I could knock, and Gran didn't even acknowledge me before she started peering over my shoulder at the car.

"That isn't the cute policeman."

"Ahh, Zach isn't that bad."

"That's Zach? Good. I have some—"

I put my hands on her shoulders and turned her. "Nope. No terrorizing the police until they catch Bryan's killer. Then you can chase Zach down to your heart's content." That earned me a glare, but she stopped fighting my grip and we both went back in the house.

"So, tell me about your date."

Nope. Changed my mind. Zach was on his own.

"There was no date. It was a protective detail."

"That's not what Olivia said."

Foiled by my own plot.

"It was a joke. I was teasing Brecken." I frowned as I remembered the conversation.

"Blew up in your face didn't it?"

"Boy did it. He saved a dog! Jumped into the bay and saved a dog. I didn't think he could get any sexier, but that did it. No, if he rode, he would be the perfect man." Then again, I had already tried that once. "I take that back. Just have him buy me ponies and I will be his for the rest of my life."

"Your sarcasm isn't appreciated."

"You started it. You know I don't want to date!"

"You are too young to curl up and die just because one man was a jackass!"

"I am not!" Wait. That came out wrong. "I am not

curling up and dying. I am raising my child! I can't be introducing random men into her world! What if one is a pedophile? I have horrible taste in men! Look at my ex. No. I have to think of her. No men. No dating."

"This is your father's influence."

"Not everything that you dislike about me is my father's fault."

"This is. This idea of being perfect in everything you do to the exclusion of anything else." She shook her head. "You don't have to be perfect, and there's no reason that you can't date *and* be a good mother, too. Who knows? The man you find might be a good influence on Hailey. One she desperately needs since her father isn't going to give it to her."

"Gran! You know we don't talk bad about Blake. Even when Hailey isn't here. It makes a habit."

"This isn't talking bad. This is talking real. And he really has no interest in being a large part of that child's life other than being the 'fun dad.' He doesn't want to parent. So, go find someone else who will."

"I'm confused. So now I'm dating for Hailey? Or the town?"

"And yourself. And any other babies that might come along." Ding, ding, ding. We had a winner.

"You want more grandchildren."

"*Great*-grandchildren."

For the love of pancakes. I sighed.

"Who's pregnant?"

"Sally Mae's granddaughter. With her second. I mean, I still win because I have mine right here and hers are down in Los Angeles, but it would be nice to have another."

Sweet cheese and crackers.

"Go bother Janet. She hasn't had any."

"Goodness, no. Just think of the man she might bring home."

"I brought home Blake! The cheating, demeaning asshat that—"

"Tsk, tsk. I thought we weren't insulting Blake even when Hailey isn't home."

Insane. Everyone in this town was insane. I rubbed my face, trying to hide the reality that was my family.

"Maybe if I hang around my house and ask nicely, the murderer might kill me, too."

"Oh! That's a good idea. You go there right now. I'll distract Zach." She turned to go back to the front door, leaving me gaping in her wake. What just happened here? I expected her to call me crazy. Or a drama queen. Not help me follow through on a plan that even I admitted was ridiculous. Was she trying to make fun of my over-the-top melodrama?

Nope. She was out the door. What's happening here?

I ran after her.

"No, Gran. I am not letting you bully Zach into buying your tea. Even as a distraction. And why were you distracting him?"

"So, you could sneak out. Although, we should have a better story for Brecken when I call to tell him."

I was going to regret asking this.

"Why are we calling Brecken?"

"So he can save you! It's so romantic." She sighed, and her eyes lost focus as she planned out my imaginary rescue.

"One day I'm going to learn to stop being sarcastic." I was getting a headache. A grandmother-sized headache.

"That's not going to happen, dear. Just like Janet's never going to pick a good man for herself. It's just not in your nature." She gave me a pat on the arm and then dragged us both back in the house.

"I feel like I should protest that last statement."

"Don't bother. I have the facts on my side." She released me when we walked into the kitchen. "Do be a dear and finish the cookies over there. Alice is bringing some of her own, and we have to show her who's the better baker."

"Olivia is," I mumbled under my breath while I obediently went to the counter where all the ingredients were laid out. Chocolate thumbprint cookies with walnuts. I knew this recipe by heart, and it was my culinary masterpiece. I sensed matchmaking here. I debated refusing, but one glance told me that fighting Gran on this would just make her resort to another scheme. At least in this one I got cookies.

Two hours and one guard change later, we were getting ready to leave for Judy's house when Brecken drove up.

"Can I give you ladies a ride?"

"Is that an offer or a request?" I asked him.

"Lark! Where are your manners? That would be lovely, Brecken. Thank you." Before I could protest, Gran gave me a glare that started in her eyes then traveled to her chin, which jutted out. Message received. Get in his freaking car. I saluted her like a soldier and opened the door to the backseat. "No! No. Lark, you should take the front seat."

Chocolate and wine. Chocolate and wine. One short little drive and I would have chocolate and wine.

"Have you ever had chocolate thumbprint cookies, Brecken? My Lark made them from scratch today." Brecken looked over at me with a grin as he helped Gran put the cookies in the trunk with her other food.

"I can't say that I have, but I look forward to the experience."

"Oh! Are you staying for the Sewing Circle? How wonderful," Gran added, beaming at him.

Laying it on a little thick over there, Gran. Back it up.

"Yep. I *volunteered* to be Lark's protection at the Sewing Circle."

Oh no. He obviously meant something by that. And I'm pretty sure it wasn't him wanting to be there for a bunch of old women gossiping... That sly dog. He was using me to interview the gossip queens without them being suspicious!

"You're using me to talk with the Sewing Circle!" I hissed at him while we waited for Gran to get in the car. She was taking forever to... sigh. This was the last straw. I was never dating in this town again. Not that we were dating.

I was in so much trouble.

Brecken just smiled back at me before turning his attention to Gran.

"Elise, is there anything I can do to help you? I know that getting into such a small car can be hard. I groan every time I get in. Here, let me help you." He rushed over to assist her, carefully helping her in like a gentleman from a Victorian-era movie.

"Oh, please," I groaned as she sat down, beaming up at him.

"See, Lark! Some men have manners. They know how to treat a woman," Gran commented from the back seat.

"I'm going to stick with 'oh, please.'"

Gran and Brecken talked most of the way there. She dug into his past, his parents, where his sister was living. How she liked it there. Did he think she might like small-town living better? Subtle, Gran, real subtle. Halfway through the trip my head dropped to my hands to escape and stayed there until we reached John and Judy's house. Sally Mae and Alice were already there, waiting by the door for us to show up. I glanced over the seat at my grandmother in time to see her slipping the phone in her pocket. Sneaky old bat.

"Lark! Elise! Come in! Come in!" Sally Mae said as she walked towards us. It wasn't even her house, but she was acting like the hostess. "And who's this charming addition? It isn't often that men have the gumption to take on all the old biddies."

I winced but introduced him anyway. It was too late for him to run now. "Sally Mae, Alice, this is Brecken Wilson. He's the detective that has been working with John on Bryan's case." Sally Mae stepped in front of Alice to reach her hand out, palm down. Did she really think he was going to kiss it? Oh, please! She wasn't old enough to expect that. I was pretty sure that she was born after 1900.

"Pleasure to meet you, Sally Mae." Brecken took her hand and *kissed* it. Just like in the movies. Did they bring back The Twilight Zone and not tell me they were filming it here? This was getting ridiculous.

Also, how did I get a kiss on the back of my hand? Or other places...

"What a gentleman!" Sally Mae tittered. Yeah, yeah. Everyone knew Brecken was chivalrous.

"Alice." Brecken turned to her and took her hand, giving her the same kiss. "It's nice to see you again. I can't wait to catch up later." She swallowed hard and ripped her gaze from his chest to his face. I couldn't judge. He had been ridiculously handsome when he was glaring at me before this. Kissing hands and giving compliments with his dreamy eyes? Devastating.

"Shall we go in?" I threw out. I was over this. He was hijacking my idea, and I was not happy about it.

"Sure." Alice and Sally Mae led the way, Gran tucked in between them as they gossiped. About me, no doubt.

"*What the fish sticks!* What are you up to, Casanova?" I hissed at him.

"*Fish sticks?* Is that in place of hell? Or the F-word? Your non-swearing is different."

"Does it matter?" I said it a little too loud; the older ladies turned around to look back at us, and I waved at them with a tight smile. Nothing wrong over here. Just me going crazy. "Why are you kissing their hands?"

"Because it makes them like me."

"So?"

"If they like me then they'll share their bounty of knowledge."

"And John just can't ask Judy because—"

"She doesn't know anything. And she won't bring it up because they don't talk about John's work at home. It's a rule in their marriage that they keep their home lives and John's job separate at all times. No exceptions. I think it's stupid, but it's their rule."

From what John had told me, it was a genius rule. It was probably why their marriage was still working.

"So, they sent you in as a spy."

"John guessed they would be more interested in setting us up than caring why I was here."

John had a point.

"Fine. Let's go." I took one step before swinging back. "But get this straight—I don't need a man. I don't need to date. I'm a successful, independent woman who has priorities that don't include men." There, I told him. Except that he was smirking at me. "Why are you smiling?"

"Because I get to you, don't I?" He stepped into my space and I could smell his cologne. Nope. Just because he smelled like sandalwood and citrus, did not mean my legs should go weak. Bad knees.

"I don't know what you are talking about." I even lifted my chin a little to show him how serious I was about my denial. Then I instinctively licked my lips, which didn't help my point. But his lips were right there.

And they were so red.

"You know, as a detective, I am trained to notice things."

"Oh, please. I heard this speech on the TV. Now you are going to tell me all the 'little tells' I have that you've decided mean I'm attracted to you." I rolled my eyes. I was faking it well tonight.

"Nope. I was going to tell you that you say some of your thoughts out loud when you think. It's a common trait among people that work alone. They start talking to themselves."

Oh, fudge buckets.

No. That couldn't be a real thing. I would know if I said something.

"No, I don't!" He had to be bluffing. It was a good bluff, though.

"Hmm, no denial that there were thoughts about me." He gave me a wink and stepped away, causing me to take a sharp breath as he brushed against me on his way inside. His voice floated towards me as he sauntered to the door. "I'm going to take that as confirmation I was right. You think about me. Thoughts you don't want anyone to know."

"I do not talk to myself out loud!" I squeaked at him. "Oh, and there were no thoughts. Hear that? NO THOUGHTS!" None that were out loud, anyway. And I wasn't missing his body heat right now. Not at all. I was just cold. And he was hot. So hot.

"Well, you are being honest about one thing. You don't talk out loud. I was just saying it to see what you would deny." He entered the house, leaving the door open for me to follow. Eventually. As soon as I picked my jaw up and figured out what had happened.

Still a little dazed, I stood there for a while, staring at the open door.

"Are you going in? Or can I join you as we stare at the door? We have all been a little nervous about joining the Circle." I turned to look over my shoulder and saw Dorothy standing there.

"I'm not joining. Just thought I might hang with you guys tonight, since, well, I just thought some company would be nice."

"That's how it starts. Then, suddenly you are here every week, bringing food and complaining about men."

"No, really. I'm not joining. I just—wait. Is the complaining about men obligatory? Who do you complain about?"

"My late husband. My ex-boyfriend. My current boyfriend. Whoever is more relevant to the conversation."

Wow. I had been out-cooled by an 83-year-old. I was pathetic.

"I don't have anyone to complain about."

"Don't be silly. You have that ex of yours, right?"

"We try not to complain about him because it sets a bad example. I don't want anything to get in between Hailey and her dad."

"Complaining about him here won't do that."

"Habits. I get in the habit here and then it happens at home."

"Then go get someone new to complain about." She smirked.

"Not you, too."

"I heard something about you and a police officer," she prompted, her smile widening.

"Yeah. He came in to help with Bryan's case."

"Did we need help? I thought that's why we bamboozled John into staying."

"No." I smiled at her as she wrapped her arm in mine. "He has personal reasons. John is letting him assist."

"And is he as cute as they say?"

"Yes." It came out in a long, breathy sigh. Way to be subtle, Lark. Dorothy just raised her eyebrow at me but didn't comment. "I mean…" I had no idea how to save this. "… yes. Yes, he's gorgeous."

"And saves dogs."

The rumor mill in this town was out of control.

"And saves dogs."

"Tough situation. Perfect man, and yet here you stand. Afraid."

"I am not!" Geez Louise. What was it with people saying I was scared? I wasn't scared. I was smart. I was protecting my child. And, I was terrified.

"I can see you need some time with your thoughts. You want me to stay with you?"

"No." I wasn't a coward. "Let's go in." She nodded her approval and we entered the house.

Brecken was sitting in the center of the group, buried in food and little old ladies. Gran sat beside him, glaring at Sally Mae, who was telling him about her 'wonderful, *single* granddaughter.'

"—she lives right there in San Fran, like you!"

"Sorry, I don't think we've met. San Francisco is a big place—"

"No, no! Two people who *live so close* should meet!"

"The city is huge. We probably don't even live that close," he protested again, but she still persisted.

"I will text her right now! Give her your number."

"No, really! Please don't. That would be... too much. After all this food, I wouldn't want to take advantage of your generosity."

Ha! Nice try. Not going to work.

"No, no. You just moved there! It would be rude not to put you two in touch!" He moved to San Fran years ago! It was time to rescue him.

"Sally Mae, how's Maria doing? What is it that she does, again? Or should I say *now*? I know she was struggling finding somewhere that appreciates her... unique personality."

She glared, her lips pursing as she took a deep breath and pulled herself up. "She's a sales clerk. At Macy's. She's been there for two months already."

"Ahh." I met her eyes and challenged her to keep going. I had more. The gossip from the Sewing Circle had its uses. Oh, god. Dorothy was right. I would probably have to join. God have mercy on my soul.

Sally Mae backed down, muttering something about needing to help Judy in the kitchen. Gran followed, but not before giving me an approving look. Brecken had his smirk back, but didn't say anything, handing me a beer as I took the seat Gran had just left.

"You owe me." I took a sip of beer and looked

around, trying to ignore my awareness of where our thighs met.

"No argument here. She was relentless," he whispered, his breath tickling my neck. I let out a chuckle and relaxed into my seat, trying to act like I didn't want him to do it again. A change in topic was needed now.

"Where did you get the beer? I thought they only had wine at these things."

"Judy just handed two beers to me and winked."

"*Fudge buckets*. This better be worth it." I can't believe Judy was siding with Gran. That was disappointing. Expected, but disappointing. He grinned. I was starting to miss grumpy Brecken. Grumpy Brecken was easier to resist. But I had a daughter to get back. I had to get down to the business of solving this murder.

"Let's talk to Dorothy. She could at least give us the manager's name."

"Who is Dorothy?"

"Owner of the resort. Lives on my street a few doors down."

"Lead the way." We both got up, and I caught Dorothy's eye as we walked over.

"Hello, Dee. This is Brecken. He's a detective with the Sheriff's department. Brecken, this is Dorothy Watts, owner of the resort and savior of our town."

"Oh, please, Lark. Don't be so dramatic. I only saved, like, half the town at most." She gave Brecken her most charming smile then drew in a sharp breath as she got a good look at him.

"Pleasure to meet you, ma'am," Brecken said

politely. I expected more hand-kissing and rampant flattery, but he stayed back, quietly studying her. I waited for him to start talking again, but he just stood by my side, contemplating Dee with narrow eyes. On her part, she was just as puzzling. Gone was the warm, nurturing woman that I knew, and instead was the businesswoman. She had pulled up to her full height, her face taking on a haughty, neutral expression that was tight enough around the edges to indicate disapproval.

"Is everything okay?" I asked, flipping my gaze between them as the standoff continued.

"I didn't know that you owned the resort out here. Or that Bryan was so close to you," Brecken told Dorothy quietly. I fell silent, hoping to find out the back story.

"My husband is dead, and so are his grudges. It's over and done with."

Husband? Her husband knew Brecken? But he had been dead for years.

"Not everyone feels that way."

What was happening here? That sounded threatening.

Her jaw clenched before she pushed her head back slightly to make herself look even taller. "I didn't know Bryan was related to your family. He had nothing to do with us."

Who, or what, was 'us'?

"And the drugs he was passing through your hotel? That didn't make you upset?" Wow. He just went for it. I stared at him a second too long, alternating between being impressed and horrified. But I lingered too long, and when Dee started to speak I had to swing my head around so fast that I almost gave myself whiplash.

"There are no drugs going through my hotel."

Well, that denial sounded authentic. Too authentic. This was about to get awkward.

"We have proof that Bryan was a drug dealer, and the rumors were that he was using your hotel as a base of operations to get drugs to your customers," Brecken said quietly.

The businesswoman persona was gone, and she was back to the woman I knew. Her face scrunched up in confusion as she processed the words.

"I know that we have a dealer, and that they would occasionally meet our customers' less traditional needs, but never at the hotel. Never. There's no way it would happen underneath my nose."

Brecken handed her his phone, and she studied the photo of Bryan and the night manager for a second, then handed it back while her jaw worked back and forth.

"That traitorous bitch. I can't believe she would be that stupid." Dee's voice shook with anger. "Her name is Gina Spitz. She is the night manager at the hotel. She has worked there for the last six months after she had… conflicts with one of my son's managers about the meaning of the word 'no.' This was supposed to be her clean start away from all the drama." She looked away for a second before turning back to us. "The manager was fired, and we offered to help her press criminal charges, but she kept saying we owed her money for her pain, not jail time for the aggressor. She threatened to sue. We pointed out that she didn't have a case, but it seemed easier to help her get a new start in a new business. I guess that didn't work out so well for me."

"So, she has a personal grudge against you and your family?"

"Yes." She looked at the photo again and shook her head. "The poor thing needs to have better taste in men. If Bryan was your dealer, then he was playing a few girls. Most notably his boss."

Hold up. Laura?

"He was sleeping with Laura? And cheated on her? Again?" I exclaimed. Wow. Some women really did have horrible taste in men. Maybe matchmakers weren't such a bad idea after all.

"What's this about Laura?" Alice asked as she came up behind Dee.

"The man that was murdered. He was sleeping with Laura and my night manager," Dee told her. Sally Mae followed on Alice's heels.

"Wasn't he sleeping with that redhead we saw him with at the beach that one day?" Sally Mae asked Judy, who looked surprised.

"That was Bryan? I didn't recognize him," Judy added before turning to Brecken and continuing. "We were out bird-watching when we stumbled upon them... well, let's just say they were doing things that shouldn't be done on public beaches. But I didn't get a good look at his face."

"I wasn't looking at his face," Sally Mae commented. When we all turned to look at her with sagging jaws, she realized what we thought she meant and clarified. "His leg! I was looking at his leg. And that

Marine Corps. tattoo he had. It was definitely Bryan's."

I was stunned. I had slept with fewer men in my entire life than the women Bryan had been sleeping with right before his murder. So much for our earlier logic. I was willing to bet that the killer was a woman. I also imagined she could plead a pretty sympathetic case. All the women would vote for her to get off due to insanity.

"So, he was sleeping with three women at the time of his murder," Brecken summarized.

"Four," I murmured absently. "You're forgetting Becky."

"I'm starting to see why he was murdered," Dee commented. Alice, Judy, and Sally Mae all nodded in agreement. I turned to Brecken.

"But which one did it?" I asked.

"Or group," Judy added.

"Or group," I corrected.

"Becky was at the Pub," Dee offered. "I was there meeting one of my gentleman callers Sunday night."

"Do we even have a time of death?" I asked Brecken, realizing I didn't know when he was killed.

"Yes. It was—nope! I'm not telling you information about the case." He glared at me over his almost mistake then went back to thinking.

"Okay then." They would have needed to know my location at the time of the murder. I thought back to my schedule that day. Since they hadn't questioned me further, I must have had a verifiable alibi. "He was killed in the morning or around mid-day."

"How did you—?" Brecken's face turned pink as his lips pressed together.

"Logic, my dear Watson." I couldn't hold back my smirk.

"Then poor Becky isn't off the hook," Dorothy added, "but Gina is."

"What do you mean?" I asked.

"Gina was at church. She's a very religious girl; she never misses." Ironic.

"And then there were three." Sally Mae rubbed her hands together.

I didn't blame her. This was fun. In a sort of sick way.

"Was Laura at her shop that morning?" I asked.

"Yes. But so was Bryan," Alice cut in. "I saw them both before church around 9 a.m." I looked at Brecken. He would know the timeline.

"They both got off at 11 a.m. It didn't seem suspicious at the time," he conceded.

I snorted. "It does now. Do you know where they went?" I asked, and his eyes flashed at me. "Come on. Tell me more. I know you don't like to tell civilians, but we've discovered more in ten minutes here than you have in your whole investigation. Start telling me everything and maybe I can go home sometime soon! I don't want my house to be a crime scene anymore."

"Laura went home. Bryan went to go hiking," Brecken grunted.

"Well, that's a lie," Gran offered as she came up behind me.

"How do you know?"

"Because no one goes hiking on Sunday. The parks are closed. That, and I saw him pulling into his house before noon."

"How do you know which house is his?" he asked.

"Please!" Alice said with a sniff. "He had a huge house and no reasonable way to pay for it. We've been keeping an eye on him."

Brecken's hand went to his forehead again, and he rubbed the same spot in the center. "Did you ladies tell John or Benny about your suspicions?"

"No. Why would we? We didn't have anything concrete. So, we watched," Alice replied.

He rubbed harder.

"If your husbands ask, I didn't just learn that." They both nodded like his response made sense. That their husbands would care about Brecken knowing that they were watching… Ahh. They were doing something stupid and their husbands would be upset about it.

Blake had never cared what I did. He still didn't. Maybe that should have been the first clue that the relationship wasn't meant to be. Or that he wasn't really in love with me.

"Were there any other cars parked at his house?" Brecken asked Gran.

"A red mustang."

Well. I smiled at Brecken. We had ourselves a winner.

"But how did they cut up the body?" I asked, my shoulders drooping again. "There's no way that they would be able to cut up the body at his house. Do we think they left to go somewhere after meeting?"

"They?" Brecken questioned.

"Redhead and Bryan, of course. Oh, you mean the

first 'they.' Please. The redhead is like, five-foot-nothing. I can believe that she killed him, but moving the body? And cutting it up? That would be near impossible for her to do without attracting attention. She must have gotten help."

"Not if they did it during church. Everyone was there. Except for you, Laura, Bryan, and Becky," Gran said.

"Was that unusual?" Brecken asked Gran.

"No. Lark, Laura, and Bryan all work Sundays. Becky doesn't go because she isn't religious, so she stays late closing out The Pub so the other people can go."

"That's so sweet! She's such a sweet girl," Alice commented to Judy.

"It is. We need to find that girl a man. Someone better than Bryan. No offense, Detective," Judy responded.

I kept forgetting that Bryan was his cousin. I was glad I didn't refer to Bryan as a man-whore out loud.

"None taken. Once you sleep with multiple women at the same time, you do lose your 'good boy' title."

"Which was already tarnished," I commented. They all looked at me before Sally Mae caught on, which wasn't surprising; she was a teacher until she retired a few years ago.

"That's right! He had cheated on Laura once before. In high school." Sally Mae shook her head in disgust. "Wow. She had to have been livid."

"But did she know?" Brecken asked, pulling out his phone.

"She's one of the few people in town that follows all

of Lindsey's blogs. She pays for advertising and she wants to make sure she gets the most out of it," Judy replied.

"So, she saw the picture," Brecken commented.

"And knows our redhead girl," I added.

"And has a motive. Revenge," Alice suggested.

"No alibi." Sally Mae smiled. We were on the right track.

"The ability to cut up a body and dispose of it and then clean it up later." We all turned to Gran in surprise. "I don't know why it didn't occur to me before. Her father was an avid hunter, but he was one of those 'if you kill it you eat it' people. Since we don't have a butcher in this town, he would butcher his own meat. He got pretty good at it after a while. His equipment is still at his house. Laura never cleaned it out after he died." We all gaped at her.

She had just been sitting on this information?

"Gran?"

"Yes, darling?"

"You didn't think that would be valuable information to tell the police when BODY PARTS STARTED SHOWING UP?" I cried.

"Lark, dear. You shouldn't yell like that. It's unbecoming. I swear, Brecken, she's usually such a cool cucumber. This behavior is just because of the body parts. She has a delicate constitution."

I loved my grandmother. I loved my grandmother—

"This yelling has to be the coffee talking. Lark, you should really switch to tea," Gran added.

It was on, old woman.

Brecken caught me as I lunged to pull on her hair. One little tug in the right place and it would come down. Yes, it was petty revenge for not telling us that there was a location in town that was basically abandoned and available to cut up a body. But imperfect hair? At the Sewing Circle? Her world would end. For her part, she just smiled at me and *tsked*.

"Nice reflexes, Brecken. I have always appreciated a man with good reflexes."

She was certifiably crazy.

"Hello? Is anybody here?" My aunt came walking in the door, actually carrying fabric, unlike everyone else. Nice to know someone tried to at least sew something. "What's this?" She dropped her fabric as her hand flew to her mouth when she took us in. "Oh, Lark! I knew it. I just knew it! From the moment you brought him home, I knew he was The One."

I looked around. We were all gathered in the entryway, me in Brecken's arms, which were still wrapped around my waist from holding me back. I hadn't even noticed that they were still around me. They just felt too good. Too natural. Like we fit together. *Uh oh, spaghetti-o*. I squirmed until he let go, and then I walked as far as I could get before addressing her.

"It isn't what it looks like."

"Oh, Lark. So proud. It's okay to like a man. So, you are divorced. And your ex cheated on you multiple times. And you have a daughter. Some men like that."

Oh. My. God.

"Brecken? Can you drive me home?"

"You think that's a good idea?" he asked.

"I think if I stay here, I might kill one of them."

"Don't say things like that to the police. Just think them very, very hard."

"Noted."

CHAPTER 15

I ended up driving Brecken's car home so he could text and let John and the team know about our new lead. Since I wanted to have my life back before my child forgot who I was, I was happy to drive. I pulled into my driveway before realizing I didn't know if it was okay to stay here.

"What's the plan, Stan?" I asked as I stared at my house. It was weird. Despite the body parts and the craziness of the last few days, this was still home. Which was strange, to be honest. I would have thought after the first body part I would have been out. But I wasn't. This cottage, this town, as much as they frustrated me, were home.

And... it had a light on.

Could I have left a light on? No, I hadn't even been in the living room long enough to turn on a light. Did the police? Was that a MOVING SHADOW? I hoped I was just paranoid.

"Brecken," I hissed. He was still staring down at his phone, typing furiously and trying to coordinate whatever. "Brecken! Someone's here."

"No, those are just the cops watching your house.

We have one set of them two houses down from what I saw when we drove up. The rest of the cars are ones that were here earlier." I watched as he checked in the rearview mirror to confirm, but he didn't look at the house. That was supposed to be secure. Because people were watching it. I blew out a long breath. I had to be imagining things. Maybe the stress of the situation was getting to me.

Nope.

No, I was pretty sure there was movement.

"You sure that no one is in the house? Because I am pretty sure I didn't leave a light on."

That got him. He looked up and homed in on the light in my living room.

"You're sure that you didn't leave any lights on?"

"Yep. I turned them all off when we left. And the only light I had turned on before we left was the kitchen. Could someone on your team have left a light on?" We caught the shadow again, passing the window as we watched. I turned to Brecken and lifted my eyebrows.

"Okay. You're right. Someone's in there."

"No kidding, Sherlock."

"After this is done, we're talking about your Sherlock obsession."

"Please. These days everyone is obsessed with Sherlock. Deal with it."

"Okay. Here's what's going to happen. *You* are going somewhere safe. Maybe your grandmother's? I already called in back-up. Take this car and go."

"Okay. Is there any risk to the house I am going to?" I was watching him carefully and saw his hesitation.

Yeah. Not going to Gran's house.

"I wouldn't go anywhere that's normal. Just in case." So not Jen's. And not Gran's, either. The barn. I could go to the barn. The barn apartment would work. No one was at the barn.

"I'm going to my barn. Call me when the house is safe?" He nodded. He got out just as John approached quietly in his own car. Jogging back, Brecken got into John's vehicle and it went back to being silent. Oh. They were waiting for me. I pulled out and made my way to the barn, stressing about how much damage my house could endure. I prayed there would be no bullet holes. Or damaged furniture. Or damaged pictures. Oh god. There were so many ways this could go wrong.

I pulled into the barn parking lot, driving back to the living quarters area. Shifting the car into park, I grabbed my purse and paused mid-lean. *Dagnabit*. The barn doors were open. *Snickerdoodles*. Billy always closed them after the night feeding. Always. I bet one of the boarders left them open. Putting my purse back down, I grabbed my phone to use the flashlight and noticed a text from Jen.

Jen: *I heard you went on a date with the hot detective. I didn't know there was a hot detective. We need to talk about your sharing skills.*

Me: *Sorry. I have been...*

Oh lord. I didn't know what I had 'been.' Trying to ignore him? Pretending he wasn't making me wake up and notice that he was attractive? How his sense of humor stirred things in me I thought were dead after my divorce? Trying to ignore how his hands sent sparks through my body, or how his lips tempted me to ignore my caution? Was it even caution? Or were they right? Was it...fear?

Delete. Delete.

Me: *Sorry. Telling you would have made it real. My feelings. Everything. And I wasn't ready.*

Send.

Jen: *Fine. You are forgiven. But we are going to talk.*

Me: *Fine. Tomorrow morning.*

Clicking on the flashlight, I got out of the car and headed over to the barn, grabbing one door before I heard Twice. She was snorting and kicking the wall. I hesitated, listening for another kick. And then another. Was she kidding me? If she injured herself kicking the wall, I was going to kill her. Or if she ruined my barn. Stupid bratty mare.

I stomped in two steps before I saw a shadow dodging towards my tack room. I froze. *Fudge balls.* Again? I had to be setting a record.

"Hello?" I called out before I thought about it. Stupid. Now they knew I was there. Why did we always yell 'hello'? If they were here innocently, they wouldn't be slinking in the shadows.

In fact, why was I here? I should have called the cops. I should have gone somewhere safe. That was the smartest way to go. Twice kicked the door again with a snort. *Shoot.* Stupid mare. Stupid trainer. In the middle of a break-in, who actually debated saving a mare from injuring herself because the mare was too irritable to deal with strangers? Chestnut mares. Never, never again. Twice kicked even harder. Darn it. I had to save the brat from herself. This was the worst decision in a long list of bad decisions.

I inched along the barn until I got to the lights and flicked them on. Nothing. This was stupid. So stupid. I was setting the record for stupid. I—

A noise from the tack room caught my attention and made it past my fear.

My saddles! *Fudge buckets*. Those saddles cost a fortune. Someone was trying to steal my saddles!

I charged towards the tack room, hesitating to glance at Twice before continuing. Other than upset, she looked fine.

"I have a … gun! I have a gun! Come out of there now!" Wow. I needed more practice at bluffing.

"Lark Davis doesn't have a gun. Unassuming, sweet, accomplished, *pretty* Lark Davis would never have anything so brazen."

Laura? What the hell?

Wait, UNASSUMING? That's what people thought of me? I was unassuming?

Laura stepped out of my tack room, and I was relieved to see no knife. My saddles might be okay.

That's when I registered the gun. Well, my bad plan just got worse. Good going, Lark. What was I thinking, again? Oh, I had to save my mare. And my saddles. If I got out of this, I needed to look into my priorities. Again.

"Drop the phone." Shoot. I hadn't called anyone.

Maybe she wouldn't notice me placing a quick call right then. Without looking at it I pressed unlock and called the first number. Which should be John. Please be John. If it was John, I promised to start calling the police before I walked into suspicious places.

I dropped it. It landed face-down, but I saw it connect right before it landed. Someone was there. Bless the horse gods.

"What do you want?" I asked her.

"I don't know. Revenge, maybe?" She shrugged as if it was nothing. Was she demented? Had we all missed some sign of mental illness? Who brought a gun to someone's place of work for 'revenge, *maybe*?

"Revenge for what?" She started walking towards me and I echoed her movements back. Nope. I was not getting near the crazy lady.

"He asked you out right in front of me, you know. He said it was to cover up our relationship. That it would be weird if he didn't ask out the hottest girl in town."

He thought I was the hottest— that was not important at the moment.

"He did it twice, but he flirted with you every time you came in. And you! You didn't care. Didn't even notice. I loved him! I worshiped him! And he wanted you. And you didn't even care!" she continued.

Huh. The body parts might have been meant for me after all. Fascinating.

Oh my god. I was going to die because I kept getting distracted in the middle of life-or-death situations.

"I'm sorry?" Okay, some psychology training would have been helpful. How to talk down the scorned murderer of a guy who liked me. Maybe that was a class in college. My dad might have been right, then. Maybe I should have gone after all.

"You will be!" Her scream hit a high note and I cringed, expecting the shot. Instead it seemed to surprise her, and she pulled herself back, trying to compose herself. "You and those other bitches. Fiona will be caught red-handed with evidence while breaking into your house tonight." She smiled at me and swung the gun around carelessly in her hands. "Gina already got what's coming to her, that faithless bitch. Do you know she knew about me and Bryan? We were friends. Or so I thought. Until I saw that photo on Lindsey's blog. Then I was drinking in The Pub when I saw him with that skank. Becky. She looked so happy. So clueless. Just like me. I thought about just sending her a note. Telling her everything. But she slept with him. He let her stay over at his house. Did you know that? He was with her at night after her shift. We never slept over." Her gun was swinging again as she used her hands to talk.

I swallowed. Plan—I needed a plan!

"I had to face the fact that I was like the others. He slept with Fiona to get better drugs to sell. He slept with me to keep his job and so I would turn a blind eye to his drug dealing. He slept with Gina for access to the resort. Only Becky didn't have anything to give him. He just liked her. And you. You were his dream girl."

Oh, no…

"What did you do to Gina?" I asked. She was almost standing on my phone. At least someone else will hear her confession.

"I visited her before I came here. She won't be stealing anyone else's man again."

Oh, god.

"But I wasn't supposed to be here." Why would she come here if I wasn't supposed to be here?

"Part of the reason he liked you was your job. Working with majestic horses. Owning your own business. Being so successful in San Francisco. I was just a cafe owner. I just took my cafe over from my parents. Not as impressive as you."

"So, you were going to ruin my stuff." Brat.

"The lock on your tack room is pathetic. One little snip with bolt cutters and I was in. But then you showed up. And now I'll have better revenge." She had moved into the center of the barn and was so focused on her rant that she wasn't paying attention to the horses. Most had sensed my panic and reacted like the prey animals they were. Bob was watching me while pacing in his stall. Twice had fallen silent for once, waiting for me to tell her what to do. Great. The mare fought me at every stage, but now she was willing to listen...

"So now you're going to kill me? Because Bryan liked me? How cliché." Think, Lark, think. I needed to push her. "I expected better than this from you, Laura. This is more something that Lindsey would do. Brash. Impulsive. *Tsk, tsk*. I mean, the body drop thing was okay. It would have been better if you had set me up for the murder. Killed two birds with one stone. Why didn't you?" I had slightly moved into her space, pushing her towards Twice. The mare, true to her personality, flattened her ears at the intruder. *Hold, girl. Hola.* I tried to send confident vibes, just like I did when she was a baby and we were trying to catch her in pasture. *I am the leader. Follow my lead, you overly aggressive monster.*

"You won't think anything when you're dead." Her face contorted, her upper lip jutting out to meet her scrunched-up nose. It wasn't a pretty look on her.

"See? Cliché. Do you want me to wait while you come up with something better? No, no hurry. It might take you a while." I tried to seem unconcerned as I slipped slightly closer to her, driving her back into Twice's stall. Twice had her head as low as it could get while still hanging out the door. Her ears were pinned so tight they looked like a part of her neck, and her upper lip was curled. I could even hear the angry swish of her tail as she jerked it back and forth. She was ready. Now I just had to push her over the edge.

I screamed.

That was the last straw. Laura, her back towards the stall, never saw the mare coming. Twice, true to her temperament, attacked, biting into Laura's gun arm. Good girl. Perfect aim. And that was why you didn't mess with chestnut mares. Booyah.

Laura dropped the gun, and I dove for it as she tried to shake off the stubborn mare attached to her arm. Diving through the air, I was almost to the gun. My fingertips were so…close….

No.

I missed.

The gun hit the ground and discharged. *Fiddlesticks!*

I hit the ground, frantically praying that none of my horses had been hit. All were fine. Well. Most were now bucking and freaking out like someone just *fired a gun* next to them, but that was to be expected. My roof now had a bullet-sized hole, though. *Fudge buckets.*

Laura managed to pry her bloody arm out of Twice's mouth and was turning to try and attack my horse as I looked at her. Oh, hell no.

I surged up from the ground, pulling my arm back to punch her. "Leave." Hit. "My." Hit. "Horse." Hit. "Alone." Laura dropped to the ground, crying and holding her face. I waited until I was sure that she wasn't getting back up before I assessed my hand. Which hurt. A lot. *Sweet cheese and crackers!* I should have asked Brecken how to punch people when I first realized I had no idea. Oh, *god* that hurt.

Focus. I needed to tie up Laura. Horsewoman style. I grabbed my phone on the way to the feed room.

"Hello?" I said into the phone. I did call John. Go me.

"Lark? Thank god. Brecken is minutes out. We'll be there soon." John's voice jumped out of the phone, and I breathed out in relief.

"Take your time. I got this."

A minute later, Laura was tied up in baling twine with her hands behind her back and her feet tied together. Just like I had seen in the movies, and I was proud of myself. I sat back to take in my work when my brain went to my next problem.

"John? I don't suppose anyone will pay to fix my

roof?" He laughed. That wasn't comforting. I stared at the hole. I mean, it was small. And it wasn't like we got that much rain. Then again, I did not want puddles in the middle of my walkway. Sigh. More money. Being the distraction for a murderer was expensive. Or killers. I still wasn't clear on that. I looked over at Laura. Well... we did have the time.

"So was Fiona in on it, or not? I'm a little confused on that point." Laura scowled, pressing her lips together. She wasn't talking. Too bad. "That's okay. I'm sure Fiona, or *Fee,* will talk once she learns you set her up." Yeah, I connected those dots. She had mentioned Fee with Shifty at the coffee shop. I might have just connected them a few seconds ago when I said Fiona's name out loud, but Laura didn't need to know that.

"Bitch." Laura spit at me.

I didn't think I needed a clarification on who. It didn't matter.

CHAPTER 16

It took Brecken and the cops about five more minutes to get to the barn. We both heard them coming, and Laura made one more attempt at breaking the baling twine, which ended with swear words and probably a little blood. I wasn't sure. It wasn't my problem, and I was still sore over the hole in my roof. And my swollen hand, which I had wrapped in one of the horse's ice packs as we waited. I was pretty sure I hadn't broken it. I hoped I hadn't, at least.

Even though I knew they were the rescue team, both Laura and I winced as they came through the door. Guns out and searching for a target, men in uniforms and vests flooded my barn. The horses, most of whom had just settled down from the gunshot, were now spooked again. Except Twice. She nickered at Brecken and preened as if she knew she was the hero and wanted him to come praise her. Shameless flirt.

What was worse was that he went over there and rubbed her. And she let him! It didn't matter that she had just saved my life, I wanted her to greet me like that! I wouldn't turn down him greeting me that way, either. I would be lying if I said I couldn't use a few strokes right now.

That was when the last of my adrenaline gave out. I was so tired. I slumped, praying they didn't need anything. But… manners…

"Hey, guys. Laura is there. Do you need a knife to cut the baling twine?" I wasn't going to bother getting up, but one of the boarder's horses decided he'd had enough and started kicking their stall door. Ignoring the cops as they started cordoning off my barn with police tape, I went to the horse and calmed him down before checking for any injuries. He was fine. Good. I didn't need to call—

Son of a Monkey. I had to contact all the boarders and tell them what had happened. This was not going to look good. I turned and took everything in. "*Dagnabit.* I'm not going to be able to work tomorrow, am I? Can I at least come and turn out the horses? They're going to go insane if they don't get to blow off a little steam." Brecken gave me a long look, using what I was now calling his 'police face': expressionless and professional. I was expecting a sarcastic 'no.'

"I think we can manage that." My hero. I collapsed against the wall, giving him a thumb-up gesture, and waited for them to need me again. After I was seated, it occurred to me that I might have just contaminated their crime scene. Oh well. It was too late now.

Brecken nodded, and went to talk to another cop. After they were done speaking, he drifted over to me. "You can go home now. Everything is safe and your house is fine. Fiona was just lying in wait for you to come home."

Yeah, that was comforting. Not.

"Okay. Do you want me to leave your car here and go home with one of the other cops?" He looked at me for a second, studying my face before he spoke.

"No, you take it and go home. I'll come pick it up tomorrow morning."

"Okay." I started to pull myself up when his hand was suddenly dangling in front my face, offering a lift. I looked up in surprise, but his face was still in professional mode. Well, okay then. I took his hand, letting the heat of his warmth sink into me before he pulled me up. He didn't say anything once I was on my feet, even though I hesitated to give him the chance. It wasn't until I was a few feet away that he said anything.

"Lark?"

I turned so I could see him, although he was still looking away. More specifically, he was just standing there looking at the ground. Why?

"I'm glad you're okay. I'm sorry we didn't protect you better." Oh. He felt guilty.

"No one could have known that Laura would go off the rails today. It wasn't your fault." I turned and left. Honestly, I was tired, and unless he was going to tell me how pretty I was and that he couldn't live without me, I wasn't interested in whatever he had to say. I spent the drive back going over every stupid decision I had made, starting from not calling the cops when I found the door open, to going in to save a horse that ended up saving me, to my blind rush when I thought my saddles were in danger. Seriously, I needed to rearrange my priorities.

***

The next morning, I slept in, waking at eight o'clock before calling Blake and asking him when I could pick up Hailey. She still wanted to go to the festival, but Sunday worked out just fine. Ten minutes of talking to her reassured me that she was happy, healthy, and still loved me. I hung up, relieved. I was alive (albeit barely), and Hailey was coming home. Life was good.

Twenty minutes later I had changed my mind. I had two boarders threatening to pull their horses out of the barn. I didn't really blame them. Bullets would be my line in the sand, too. In my attempts to reassure them, I ended up promising one that I would show her warmblood in third level by the end of the show season. He was barely at second. I guessed I was still channeling some of the stupid from last night, because that would be near impossible. I had a lot of work to do and very little time to do it. The next few months were going to be hectic. I had just gotten off the phone with the last boarder when Brecken knocked on the front door.

"Hello, Detective. Would you like some coffee?" Or dinner? Maybe a real date? Not to leave?

Reel it in, Lark.

"No, thank you. I'm good."

Well, that seemed to have answered all my questions nicely. My stomach seemed to drop about three inches. That had to be the first time I was disappointed to hear that phrase.

"What can I do for you?" This earned me an eyebrow in the air. Oh! Right. The car. I lifted my hand to stop his answer and went to get his keys. He walked in the house as I retrieved them, and I met him in the entryway to give them back.

"Thank you for letting me borrow it."

"Anytime." Which meant never again since he was going to be in San Francisco soon.

"Anything else?" I had plans. Some ice cream eating. Maybe even a romantic cry movie. I took him in one more time. Maybe some chocolate, too. And a beer. Two. Definitely two.

"We got most of her confession on tape from the phone. Is there anything that we missed?" He shifted his weight as he asked, and I turned and led him into the kitchen while I answered. Maybe I would have some more coffee.

"No. Pretty much everything was verbal. She made the mistake of getting too close to Twice. Took a chunk out of her arm." I fiddled around the kitchen before taking a seat at the kitchen table, looking for something to fiddle with. Anything to distract me from how I was fearing this conversation would end.

"Interesting. I didn't know horses were aggressive animals." Brecken followed close on my tail and took a seat next to me at the kitchen table.

"Any animal can be aggressive when threatened. But she might have been encouraged by my scream. Who knows? Bite isn't a command I teach." Yeah, that was how to get a man. With sarcasm and snipes. I guess we knew why he was leaving.

"And the wounds to Laura's face?"

"She turned and tried to punch Twice. So, I

punched her. A few times. Not sure how many. It was so fast."

"Got it." He put down his notebook and looked up at me. "Are you ready for everything?"

"Probably not, but let's go for it anyway."

"We were right. Fiona Miller was the redhead with the red mustang. She's a member of a drug syndicate that had been selling drugs to Bryan for years. A few months ago, he approached her with a plan to increase sales through the hotel. He outlined a plan that would allow him to get close to the night manager at the resort. He told Fiona that the manager was resentful of the owner and wanted to get back at her, so the manager was jumping at the chance to help him. Fiona had doubts. She wouldn't give him more drugs unless he could prove the buyers were real, so he seduced her instead. Fiona insisted that she thought he loved her until Laura found her and told her the truth. They confronted him at his house, and it got out of hand. She says Laura struck the fatal blow, but we'll see what Laura has to say."

"And Gina?"

He looked down at his notes and then away before meeting my eyes again. "She didn't make it. John called in a wellness check when he heard Laura mention her. They found her dead from a gunshot to the chest."

"Doesn't seem worth it, does it?" Why didn't I have coffee? I needed coffee.

"What?" He looked up at me in confusion, and his gaze held me still.

"She loved him. I'm guessing she never stopped. That's what made Laura such an easy target. She wanted the love story she didn't get the first time. Doesn't really seem worth it." Jaded, party of one. But it was true. Love left you vulnerable. It left you open to hurt. The kind of hurt that caused two women to kill their lover in a fit of rage. The kind of hurt that made a person wake up to what they were missing and then watch it go back to the city.

"Hey! Don't go blaming love for this." Brecken reached over to put his hand on mine, making me look at him. "Fiona isn't exactly innocent. We ran her prints. We already have three requests for extradition. This isn't even the first time she's been implicated in murder. And Laura had a history of mental illness. You're right. She had never gotten over her crush in high school. Started seeing a therapist soon after. Her parents were livid when they found out she gave him a job, but she said she was over him, and this was her way to prove it to them. As the years passed, they started to believe her. I think seeing him cheating on her again was too much."

"Wow." That was a lot to take in. Especially with his hand on mine.

"So no, love had nothing to do with what happened." He looked like he wanted to add something, but at the last minute his mouth slammed shut, and he stopped meeting my gaze, staring instead at where our hands touched. Ahh. I remembered this. This was where he would tell me that we're breaking up. Not that we were together. I guess it would be more accurate to say that this was where he was going to tell me he was leaving. My stomach clenched, and I followed his lead, staring down at the table, pulling my hand back and folding them in my lap.

"Do you want some coffee? I want some coffee." He looked up at me and smiled. I hesitated before my nerves got to me and retreated to the coffee maker.

"I will still pass on the coffee. I have to leave for the city after we talk." There it was. He was leaving. I said the first thing that came to mind.

"And get gas." I winced. I should have filled it up for him. That was what responsible adults did when they borrowed a car. I hadn't thought about it this morning. He stood and walked over to where I was, a soft smile on his face.

"I plan to." His amusement faded as he looked around again.

Yeah, we needed to just pull off this band-aid.

"Well, it was nice meeting you." I held my hand out, shoving it in between us for the farewell shake. But he didn't take it. After a few seconds I let it fall, looking away. God, this was painful. "Thank you for filling me in on the case. Have a good drive home." I started to walk past him when he grabbed my hand. I turned, already frustrated with his silence, when he spoke.

"I can't stay here."

"Okay."

"I really can't."

"I really didn't ask you to," I reminded him with more snap than I had wanted. We hadn't been on a date. We were nothing to each other. Just a 'what if' to remember one night over drinks. Something to remind us that the chance was there. This was painful, and awkward, and, well... awkward. But it wasn't as bad as I thought it would be. Here was rejection in all its ugly glory. Gran was right. I was hiding behind my daughter. Maybe even hiding behind my divorce. Captain America might not be Mr. Right, but he had reminded me that Mr. Right was out there. I was okay with letting him go, letting him walk away. Well, 'okay' might be overstating it a little, but I could deal. He was leaving.

"I want to stay longer. Because of you."

Well. *Fudge buckets.* I felt like I was trying to breathe through fog. My gasping was the only sound I could hear for a second while I tried to process the words and make sure I didn't just imagine them.

"What does that mean?" I whispered. Hope sat like a clamp on my heart. Could—

"I don't know."

"That's the stupidest evasion I have ever heard."

He laughed, touching my face gently as he moved closer to me, staring into my eyes.

"How about I text you?" he asked, his eyes searching mine. "Maybe the next time you're down we can go get that pho?"

"I can do that."

Well, look at that. I had a possible date. For sure, this time. I smiled at him, and he smiled back. I was still scared, but so was he. Maybe, if we went slow, he could be Mr. Right after all.

Continue reading the Lark Davis Mysteries
in Stir Up.

WANT MORE BARROW BAY?

Visit me at AnnabelleHunter.wordpress.com and sign up for my newsletter to get a free short story.